SHILLING & FLORIN

BOOK TWO:
THE THIEF & THE MARQUIS

KATE HALEY

ISBN: 978-1-991364-00-5 (paperback)
978-1-991364-01-2 (kindle)
978-1-991364-17-3 (hardcover)

Cover design by Kate Haley

CONTENTS

Visit **www.katehaleyauthor.com** for
deals and current news from the author.

1

The key grated in the lock. She didn't try and run. There was no point. Charm had been worse than useless. The sunlight through the window was broken into even shafts of cold and damning light by the iron bars. He stepped haughtily into the room. She didn't turn. Her fingers held the candle carefully as she dripped wax onto the paper below. With swift and nimble hands, she pressed the seal against one envelope, then the next. Each was given a moment to dry. Each sat like a shimmering midnight beetle against the cream parchment.

She took both letters, tapping the edges together neatly against the desk to keep them straight. Then she handed them to the man behind her.

"These should see your demands met," she told him.

"For your sake, they'd better," he replied, taking them from her hand.

The morning sun was warm on the sheets. It spilt through the lace curtains and stained the whole room a pale gold. Amy lounged in the bed, basking naked in the warmth and letting the light trail across her skin. She knew she should leave soon, but she didn't want to. She never wanted to leave. This was the only place she felt safe anymore. The only place she was happy, or as close to that as she ever got now.

It had been two months since Harry had been arrested. Two long, hideous months of lawyers and journalists and nosy, bloody-minded gossips. She rested her cheek on her elbow and gazed at the haze of pale light that marked the window. A hand stroked firmly down her back, massaging the stress from her spine.

"How's the book coming?" Lizzie asked, kissing Amy's shoulder.

"Not as effectively as I did," Amy sighed.

Lizzie laughed, nuzzling against her neck, her breath tickling across Amy's skin.

"I don't know," Amy elaborated. "I suppose I have a first draft… but I don't know if I'll ever be happy with it or let anyone read it."

"Writing something just for you is valid," Lizzie assured. "Not everything needs an audience."

"We don't need an audience," Amy smiled, rolling over to face her. She traced her fingers against Lizzie's cheek and down her neck, briefly hiding the scar on the side of her throat. Lizzie was understandably sensitive about that scar.

"Well, we have one," Lizzie sighed. "About half a dozen journalists followed you here this morning."

"That was brave of them," Amy commented.

"Madam Bronny doesn't take kindly to tabloids."

"No, and she had them all beaten from the gate," Lizzie admitted, climbing from the bed and donning a satin dressing gown. "There was another excerpt this morning though. A small one. On page three."

Amy shook her head against the pillows, messing her halo of auburn curls. She tried not to let it get to her. She tried not to engage. It was so hard though, so hard not to get dragged screaming and kicking into the bog of scandal.

"I don't care. I'm not reading them. The press won't get a reaction from me," she declared.

"I heard a rumour…" Lizzie started, sitting down at her dressing table, "that there won't be anymore leaks, that Harry's journal was stolen from evidence, and the lawyers can't sell anymore pieces of it."

"Stolen?!" Amy sat bolt upright. "But the trial starts next week!"

"Apparently, the thief said that any misplaced evidence would be returned for the trial, but that for the sake of a fair and just hearing, and in the name of protecting witnesses and innocent victims of circumstance, the journal would be kept secure; somewhere beyond of the realms of temptation for those to whom it had already proven too much to resist," Lizzie recounted verbatim.

Amy stared at her. Lizzie gave her a direct look. They both knew someone who spoke like that.

"I imagine there were some people very unhappy about receiving a message like that…" Amy commented.

"Oh yes," Lizzie agreed. "But rumour has it they were told that multiple leaks proved them incapable of protecting the evidence to the standard required. The Lord Chief Justice agreed, and said that as long as the journal was made available to both legal parties — in its original condition — upon request and in accordance with the law, no legal action would be taken against the thief."

"I bet Daddy loved having to step in there," Amy sighed.

"Did he say anything to you?" Lizzie asked.

"No," Amy shook her head. She didn't want to get into it. Lizzie knew things had been strained at home since Harry's arrest. She didn't need to elaborate.

Lizzie was still watching her carefully. There was a nervous and hesitant tension about her face as she fidgeted with the tie of her robe. Amy began to eye the tells.

"This might not be the best time to bring this up..." Lizzie began.

"You don't want to see me anymore," Amy blurted.

Lizzie tipped her head in an unimpressed glower.

"Don't do that," she ordered. "We've talked about it. Don't do a Charlie."

"I wasn't!" Amy protested.

"You were, Amy," Lizzie muttered. "Don't do it, and don't put words in my mouth."

Amy stayed silent. She hadn't meant to force her revelation, but she could see the tension hanging over Lizzie and had just beaten her to the punch. She was getting very sick of everyone referring to her impulsive deductions as 'doing a Charlie'. The small voice in the back of her head that occasionally tried to raise that they might have a point was repeatedly and brutally stomped on.

"I really like you, Amy," Lizzie sighed. "I really do. I like you, and I like the work, and I like getting paid, but… but when we started this… when we started it felt healthy. It felt healing… like we were helping each other. Like we were both survivors of different parts of the same nightmare. I want to keep that. Knowing you like I do… I'd rather be your friend, and have us continue to help each other heal, than become some kind of crutch for you. I don't think that would be good for us. Either of us."

"And that's what you think is happening?" Amy asked.

"I think that you come here to hide from reality, and as a means of retaliating against a host of men you're not speaking to," Lizzie replied.

Amy glared.

"Am I wrong?" Lizzie asked.

"Yes," Amy lied, climbing from the bed. "You are, but if that's how you feel, I won't waste your time."

"I'm not throwing you out, and I'm not saying I don't want to see you," Lizzie sighed. "I'm just proposing we take a break so that you can adjust to life without using me as a place to hide."

"What's wrong with that?" Amy demanded, picking her gown up from the floor and throwing it forcefully on the bed. She began to dress herself angrily. "I don't know if you've seen my life recently, Lizzie, but what in

God's name is wrong with me wanting somewhere to hide from it? I'm glad you've found our time together so healing, but, what? Now you're doing better and you don't need my interest to validate you anymore?"

Lizzie rolled her eyes. "That might actually sting if you hadn't been getting cross with me nearly every visit this past fortnight."

"I haven't!" Amy protested.

"Yes, you have." Lizzie sighed, standing and crossing over to her. She reached out, gently touching her face and kissing her cheek. "I am not trying to be smug or snide or cruel, Amelia. I'm trying to help. I'm very lucky that I've made it back to a good place now, but I can see that you're not there yet. I can see how deeply you're still hurting. I understand, really, I do. I don't know how long it's going to take you, but I do know I'm not who you really need to be seeing, and you won't talk to me about it. You just get angry every time I try and bring it up."

Amy flushed bitterly. She knew what Lizzie meant. It irritated her no end. They'd had that fight so many times now… shit. Lizzie was right, they had been arguing. But she wasn't ready to deal with it. She wasn't ready to talk about it. Was that so wrong? Why couldn't she just focus on the parts of her life she could cope with until she was ready to face the rest?

"You haven't seen him or spoken to him since your graduation party," Lizzie whispered. "I know he's not always the easiest company, but he did just steal evidence from the case to try and help protect you. He's an idiot, but it's how he shows he cares."

"An idiot?" Amy echoed. "Everyone else calls him the smartest man alive."

"Only the people who don't know him," Lizzie replied. "And given the men I know, that's really not saying much anyway." She took Amy's hands in hers and held them gently. "You don't have to talk to him about this. You can talk to him about what he's working on now, aside from the trial. You can tell him about your book. Hell, you can tell him Bronny and I sent you to ask what in God's name Julian's been up to. But whatever you choose, you should talk to him. You bring him up every week. I know he's on your mind."

"But he just left!" Amy muttered. "He got Harry arrested, had Jane and Laura stitch him up, and then he just disappeared. He never came back. Classic Shilling, right? Case closed, moving on. Why would he care what I had to say?"

Lizzie laughed, pulling Amy gently into her arms and kissing her cheek.

"Oh Amy, for two peas in a pod, you really don't know him that well, do you?"

"What's that supposed to mean?"

"You'll see." Lizzie squeezed her warmly.
It didn't feel like they were fighting anymore, but Amy wasn't sure if that meant they were still breaking up. Did it count as a breakup if their relationship was professional? It should. It should be a breakup. It should feel more personal. She should be more upset. God, it felt like all her time was spent these days trying to work out how she should feel. At least it sounded

like Lizzie was still prepared to see her, even if it was only with their clothes on.

2

The walk home was short but tedious. Everywhere she went now she was accompanied by a parasol, no matter the weather. It helped to block her from photographers. More often than not these days she was travelling by carriage just to avoid the attention, but she missed being able to walk around the city without being harassed.

Someone was waiting by the gate as she came up the street. She didn't know their names, but she was starting to recognise faces. She turned her parasol to block him as he raised his camera. The flash went off, but she was safely covered. It was almost strange they persisted.

"Miss Florin!" he called, ambushing her she strode up the pavement. "Miss Florin, do you have anything to say regarding the excerpt published this morning?"

The front of a camera was shoved under her parasol. She drove it down as the flash went off again.

"It's Doctor Florin, and I can't imagine I have anything to say to someone who can't even determine that," she retorted, trying to push by him.

"So you have no comment concerning Pound's claims that you made him kill those women?!" the reporter goaded, chasing after her.

Her hand paused on the gate. It wasn't the first time someone had yelled that at her. She needed to ignore it and go inside. She needed to walk away. Giving them anything else was a recipe for disaster. But she was starting to crack. Was this going to be what the rest of her life looked like? People were starting to stare, and she couldn't unfreeze. The camera shoved through again. She flinched as it flashed in her face.

Then a hand snatched it from the reporter and threw it on the ground. There were startled cries all around as it smashed across the cobbles. Amy was surprised to find she was one of them. Not as surprised as she was by the appearance of the shabby pale coat, standing firmly between her and the reporter.

"How many times do you have to be told, Lionel?" Shilling demanded.

"That's the second camera of mine you've destroyed, Mister Shilling," Lionel retorted haughtily. "And they are expensive."

"Stop sticking them in people's business then," Shilling replied. "Lord Pound warned you lot that if you didn't stop harassing his daughter, he would have you thrown in prison."

"So, do *you* have anything to say regarding the Pound scandal and your work in the arrest of Florin's fiancé?" Lionel turned his attention to the man in his face. "Is it true that the two of you were frequenting High Houses before Pound Junior was caught attacking you?"

"Prison, Lionel," Charlie grated. "Do you like England? Because if the police come knocking, there is nowhere you can go that I won't be able to find you. I'll even do it for free as a public service, you vulture."

"So, you have no interest in commenting on the rumours that you were having an affair with Miss Florin during the Jack's reign of terror?" Lionel pressed.

Shilling whistled sharply over the top of Lionel's deceitful question. He stuck his fingers in his mouth to generate the shrill sound, looking past the reporter and raising his other hand. Lionel panicked at the action and scampered away. He was halfway down the block before he realised there was no one chasing him. Shilling had bluffed hailing officers.

"Keep running, Lionel!" Charlie bellowed after him.

The man straightened his coat haughtily and stalked off. There was no point trying to come back. His camera was broken, and Shilling looked angry enough to break something else if he tried anything more.

Amy had never seen him that angry before. It was strange, she thought, given the circumstances under which she had gotten to know him. They had been hunting a serial killer, a murderer who had targeted Shilling's people, and she'd never seen him as angry as he had been staring down that reporter.

He looked… different. Aside from the shabby coat, he was neater now. His clothes seemed finer and his hair tidier, possibly even combed. She wondered if she was misremembering his scruffiness, or perhaps Rebecca had simply gotten to him recently. His anger faltered when he saw her, and the cold confidence vanished.

"Hello Florin," he mumbled. His eyes shot to the

pavement and he clutched the front of his coat for comfort, one finger carefully circling the inside of a coat button. Ah yes, that was the Shilling she remembered.

"Hello Charlie," she smiled at him, unable to help the action in response to his characteristic stimming. "You look well."

"So do you," he replied politely, staring resolutely at her shoes.

"What brings you to this neighbourhood?" she asked.

"Oh, um…" he hesitated. "Work. I'm working…"

"You have a new case?" she inquired.

He nodded, still unable to meet her eye. "Some, you know, Skipp keeps me busy…"

"What are you working on?" she asked.

He looked like he was being tortured. She almost regretted asking. Just as she was about to say he didn't have to tell her, he began to answer.

"Sterling…" he mumbled. "Lady Sterling. Hired me to find her pearls. Doing that."

"Ah," she responded coolly. "Well, I should let you get back to that then."

He didn't look up, but she could see how uncomfortable and crestfallen he looked. It sparked a small rage inside her, on top of everything else that had happened this morning. If he really didn't want to talk to her, he didn't have to.

"I'll see you at the trial, Charlie," she told him, pushing open the gate and striding up to the house. She didn't turn back to see if he had left. She didn't want to know.

Inside the house, she went straight for Henry's office. The door was ajar and she entered without knocking. Things had been different between them the past two months. He'd been different. If she was being honest, they probably both were. Nothing was the same anymore and it felt like there was nothing they could do about it.

Henry was sitting at his desk with the newspaper open when she entered. He tried to close it and hide it, and then realised it was too late and gave up, pretending he hadn't tried.

"Hello Daddy," she said softly.

"Good morning, darling," he sighed. "How are you?"

"I'm completely fine," she lied serenely. At least in regard to the paper, she genuinely hadn't seen it. "Have you seen Shilling recently?" she asked.

"No," Henry's thick eyebrows narrowed. "Should I have?"

"He was outside the gate when I arrived home. I was wondering if he'd paid you a visit," she said.

Henry shook his head. "I haven't seen Shilling since the night they arrested the Jack," he said. He never spoke Harry's name anymore. Not since that night. Now it was only ever 'the Jack', as though Harry Pound had never existed. Henry continued, "the lawyers say he's been as helpful as ever, but I don't know how much of that is sarcasm." He finally resigned himself to the task at hand and folded away the newspaper, raising an eyebrow at her. "You spoke to him?"

Amy nodded. "Briefly. He rescued me from another

of those disgraceful reporters this morning."

"How chivalrous," Henry commented drily.

"And then he lied to my face," she added.

"Lied?" Henry echoed. "I didn't know the boy knew how to lie."

"Neither," Amy sighed. "But he did. It wasn't even a good lie. I've no idea why he did it."

"What did he say?" Henry asked.

"I asked him what he was working on and he invented a fake case," Amy replied. "A bad one."

"Maybe he couldn't tell you because it was privileged, but he didn't want to say," Henry suggested.

"Maybe," Amy shrugged. "Whatever the reason, it's none of my business, and I don't think I shall concern myself with it."

Henry raised his eyebrows at her like he didn't believe her at all. She remembered Lizzie's comment from earlier, that apparently she brought up Charlie in conversation every week. That couldn't possibly be true, but clearly people were starting to develop opinions regarding her concern with the strange and scruffy sleuth. She'd have to put a stop to that.

Charlie was still cursing himself when he got to the bakery. He banged on the back door roughly. No going through the front today. Not happening. Too busy. He was sick of getting stared at and he hated people. People were awful.

Michael opened the door and looked down on him from the back step.

"Apron," Charlie announced.

Michael held his apron out by the corners instantly. It was an instinctive movement that his expression was clearly second guessing. Charlie was used to Mike second guessing everything Charlie made him do. He dug in his pockets and started emptying the broken contents into the makeshift pouch.

"Is that a camera…?" Michael asked.

"The components of," Charlie confirmed. "You can fix it?"

"Probably…" Mike stood with his arms out and the sling of his apron full of broken junk.

"Then it's all yours," Charlie told him. "You'll have to get new lenses, but otherwise yours."

"One of those days, huh?" Mike raised an eyebrow. "Why the gift?"

"Hide me in your basement for the foreseeable future," Charlie requested.

Mike grinned at him. "Sorry Sleuth, no can do."

"Please Skipp," Charlie begged. "I'll tell you what Julian's been up to."

"Don't try and play dirty, Charlie," Mike smiled. "It doesn't suit you. Susan came by this morning and asked us to keep an eye out for you today. I'm not crossing her. Just go to the wedding like a normal person."

"Have you ever been to a wedding?" Charlie sulked.

"I have," Michael nodded. "They're not bad. Rather like a good wedding."

"There's no such thing as a good wedding," Charlie huffed. "They are the most boring and tedious affairs humanity has ever indulged in."

"I bet I can change your mind…" Mike commented. He turned to the bench inside the door and tipped the broken camera parts out.

"Why? Are you my plus one this afternoon?" Charlie asked.

"I am not," Mike replied. "But I didn't put a timeframe on your conversion. I've got years to win you over."

"Congratulations," Charlie drawled. "But what do I do about today? I've already had a disastrous morning and if I go back to Rebecca and Susan now, they'll scold me."

"Why? What did you do?" Mike paused and reconsidered his question. "Whose camera did you break?"

"Lionel Tanner's…" Charlie muttered.

Michael ducked back into the building for a moment and returned a second later with a small berry pastry. Charlie's face lit up as Mike handed it to him.

"A reward for your selfless service to our community, and I'm sure your sisters would agree," he commended.

Charlie forwent replying in favour of devouring the pastry.

"So why do you think you'll be scolded?" Michael asked.

Charlie thought about replying and his chewing slowed contemplatively. There was no good way to raise it, so perhaps it was best not raised at all. The memory made his cheeks start to flush. A horrible tension curled about his stomach, and he felt a strong urge to begin cursing to himself again. Better just to focus on the glory of the pastry. Michael smirked wickedly.

"Ah," he grinned. "Lionel was going after Florin this morning. How is the good doctor?"

Charlie glared at him.

"You have a Florin face," Mike pointed. "The face you make when—"

"No, I don't!" Charlie contested heatedly.

Michael laughed. "I did think you'd scrubbed up better than normal, but I presumed that was for the wedding. So then, Becky dressed you up and sent you to see Florin this morning? She is getting meddlesome. If you saved Florin from a reporter, why are you getting scolded?"

Charlie glared at him.

"If you don't want to tell me, I can just send Swift to find out," Mike grinned. "None of the ladies turn him away."

"No," Charlie retorted. "But you might find he's a touch preoccupied at the moment. Too busy to see you yesterday and today, at any rate."

Michael's smirk faltered.

"Stings, doesn't it?" Charlie taunted.

"You said you'd tell me what he was up to..." Michael reminded.

"If you hid me for the day," Charlie countered.

"Which we both know I'm not going to do," Michael

sighed. "All right, Sleuth…" He pulled Charlie into a one-armed hug and kissed the top of his hair. "Good luck this afternoon."

"You're about to send all your runners to dig into my personal life, aren't you?" Charlie grumbled, hugging him back.

"Don't flatter yourself," Mike grinned. "I won't send them all."

"Gotta save some for Swift?" Charlie teased.

Mike shook his head against Charlie's hair. "If he was in trouble, Charlie, you'd tell me. I know you would." He let Charlie go and stepped back, glancing wistfully into the kitchen. "I do miss the old days though."

"When you were our Skipper and ordered us about?" Charlie smiled.

"I never ordered you about," Mike disagreed.

"You run us, Skipp," Charlie said. "It's why we call you Skipp. You're more sensible and organised than Swift and I put together."

"That's because when we put you two together things catch fire," Michael laughed. "Individually you're very clever. Together you share one brain cell, and it's mine."

"Rude!" Charlie laughed.

Michael ruffled his hair and they parted ways. As reluctant as he was to simply go home, Charlie knew the other options were worse in the long run. Angering Susan just wasn't worth it.

He crossed the road and came through the front door carefully, looking for traps. It wouldn't be anything messy, because Susan would be furious if Jasper got muck all over Charlie's good clothes. Whatever it was, it would be loud, probably obnoxious…

Nothing caught him in the lobby. He moved cautiously for the stairs. Something flashed out of the side doorway. Charlie snatched at it, attacking before he was attacked. Another camera hit the tiled floor and smashed loudly. Charlie sighed at the broken pieces. Someone stepped up close behind him, looking over his shoulder.

"I believe you got it, Sir," Jasper commented.

"That's the second camera I've broken today," Charlie told him. "I hope you're happy."

"It's very kind of Sir to ask after my contentment," Jasper smirked.

"Shut up, Jasper," Charlie muttered. He bent down to collect the broken pieces.

"Oh no, Sir!" Jasper exclaimed. "We can't have you—"

"Shut up, Jasper!" Charlie exclaimed. "You don't get to make work for the maids by using me. I won't have it."

"If Sir is dissatisfied with the quality of their work, I can make them work harder until you will permit them to complete their assigned tasks," Jasper taunted.

Charlie contemplated long and hard on the wrongs of physical violence and that it would be unequivocally criminal to stand up and punch Jasper in the face. Dear God, he wanted so badly to punch him. Instead, he gathered the pieces in his arms, stood, turned, and held the fractured lens up in the butler's face.

"Jasper, so help me God, go bother someone else before I shove this—"

"Charlie!" Rebecca called down the stairs.

"Shove it where, Sir?" Jasper whispered conspiratorially, a taunting smirk plastered across his face.

Charlie glowered. He left the threat open-ended and turned and stalked up the stairs. Rebecca was in her sitting room tying the finishing bow around a wrapped parcel. She looked up and eyed the parts in Charlie's hands.

"Is that Jasper's old camera?" she asked.

"Not anymore," Charlie replied. He tipped all the clinking pieces onto one of her side tables. She raised an eyebrow but looked as though it was perhaps best not to ask. Charlie kept his eyes on the broken camera, and nudged at the pieces like a half-hearted kitten.

"How was Florin?" Becky asked.

"Frustratingly hounded by the paparazzi, but otherwise she seemed well," he answered.

"Did you actually talk to her, or did you just surmise from afar like usual?" Becky judged.

"We spoke," Charlie replied.

"To each other?" Becky pressed, knowing how much of a pedant her brother could be.

"Yes, Rebecca, to each other," he huffed, rolling his eyes.

"And...?" she continued, like trying to draw blood from a stone.

Charlie flopped unceremoniously into a chair and painfully massaged the bridge of his crooked nose.

There was a small '*hrumpf*' of tortured soul.

"Ah," Rebecca sighed. "That bad."

"I don't know if she was displeased to see me," Charlie groaned behind his hands. "She was surprised. Lionel was harassing her, so I stepped in and chased him off. I think she was pleased about that, but she was surprised. Then, suddenly, I actually had to talk to her… and… well…"

"Oh dear…" Becky offered sympathetically.

"I just became so flustered," Charlie moped. "She asked what I was doing and I panicked, and I *lied* and it wasn't even a good lie! It was a terrible lie, the kind of lie that was basically a euphemism for 'I'm lying' and she knew instantly, because she's like that, and so then we were both standing there trying to pretend like I wasn't lying, when we both knew full well that I was… so then I just made excuses and ran away…"

"Oh Charlie…" Becky sighed.

"What was I supposed to do?!" he exclaimed. "Try and explain to her that I was lying because I was flustered?! Tell her that I had come by to see her and her father and ask after their wellbeing after bleeding on their carpet, and ruining her graduation party, and getting Harry arrested, and bringing down the worst scandal the city has ever seen on them, and then avoiding them for two months — because how can I possibly expect they would ever want to see me again after all that?!"

"Yes, Charlie," Becky sighed. "That is exactly what you should have said."

"That makes me sound like a lunatic!" he cried.

"No more so than everything else you say," she replied patiently.

He poked his tongue at her rudely and she returned the gesture. Sharp, crisp footsteps announced the arrival of Susan, who swept into the room like a military commander. She eyed them both, and the back of one eyebrow arched at the sight of Charlie slumped in the chair.

"Charles, I didn't realise you were back already," she commented.

"It didn't go well…" Rebecca supplied.

"That's no excuse for bad posture," Susan replied, tapping the side of her shoe reproachfully against Charlie's boot.

He slid himself very, very slowly and begrudgingly upright in the chair.

"I still don't understand why you can't just talk to the woman, Charles," Susan rebuked. "You genuinely care for Doctor Florin, it seems the simplest thing in the world to ask after her health."

"Well, Susan, there is the small compounding issue of me ruining her life…" Charlie pointed out.

"Don't be so narcissistic," Susan scoffed. "It doesn't suit you. Besides, everyone likes to know someone cares about them."

"Really? Because the last man who cared about her cared so very deeply that he brutally murdered fifteen women with features that reminded him of her," Charlie retorted.

Susan signalled him to his feet and he stood abruptly. She grabbed him by the chin and stared him in the eye.

"That man didn't care about her," she stated. "He cared only about himself. His personal vanity extended to obsession. He cared about her wellbeing only insomuch as it extended to his capacity to possess her. He didn't care if he hurt her, as long as he could own her. He held his desires above not only her health but the lives of others. That is the opposite of concern. It is selfishness, in its purest and most vile form." She paused. "You are not that kind of person, Charlie. Still, should you feel any homicidal urges come on, do let us know." She patted his cheek and let him go.

Charlie frowned slightly but didn't try and object. Susan had a good point, even if he didn't like the way she went about making it.

"Anyway, now that you're here we might as well leave early," Susan announced. "It makes sense to beat the rush, and I want to have words with Ladies Sterling and Hastings."

Charlie groaned loudly and moved to flop back into the chair. One sharp glare from Susan kept him standing, but he slumped where he stood. This was going to be awful.

3

The only real solace of weddings was that churches were interesting buildings, and everyone seemed to think it important that weddings take place in churches. The union was in glory to God, and so was the building. In her house, under her watchful eye. Charlie was sure she was glorious, our holy mother, he just wasn't sure she was real. That was something he had debated frequently with his father when he was little, before his father's illness.

His father had been a minister. A holy man. God had done nothing to save him, and nothing to save his wife when Charlie was born. Charlie's faith, insomuch as it had ever existed, had waivered further when his father died. He was certain that he had needed his father more than God did. With the evidence he had been presented thus far, it stood to reason that no one was watching, and life was only as fair as humanity bothered to make it.

Still, at least the church was nice. Even if being in church simply served to raise all these thoughts and feelings Charlie usually tried to bury. Every time he saw a pulpit, or stained glass, or gothic stonework... he missed his father. It stood to reason that he was no longer a regular attendee. Churches were for weddings and funerals, and they were full of ghosts.

They were grossly early, and his sisters were off making small talk with other guests. He couldn't think of anything to do in the immediate vicinity that could be worse. After due consideration, he was confident that he would rather have his toenails surgically removed than try and make small talk at a wedding. He knew it wasn't logical, that the surgery would be painful and debilitating and would cause a much longer period of suffering… but the illogical part of his brain was confident that it would still be preferrable.

He found himself pacing through the many rooms of the old church — at least, the ones he was allowed in. He had worked out where the family were and where the bride was preparing and he was not allowed back there, which was just fine. His footsteps always took him to the space with the fewest people, and always somewhere he could maintain a safe distance from attempts at conversation. Currently, he was back in the main room, looking at the coloured windows, and wishing that Rebecca would have let his brain have a bit of cough syrup before they left.

He glanced to the entranceway, and movement caught his eye. Suspicious movement. Charlie stepped back cautiously, trying to peer through for a better look while simultaneously positioning himself behind a pillar. A brunette man with thick sideburns was loitering by the gift table. Charlie couldn't get a good look at him from here and people kept wandering across his view. The man was looking around cautiously as he pocketed something. Charlie started forward slowly.

The man ducked away out the front door. Charlie followed. He hurried quickly and snuck by attendees, squeezing through groups of people. Too late. He burst out the front door and looked around. No sign of the man. Instantly, he turned his attention to the ground for tracks. Nothing useful. There were too many people coming and going right now, and the ground was dry. He couldn't even be certain of the man's foot size. He had been of average height, which almost certainly put him at the average foot size of most male guests. Stupid average humans. Stupid average eyesight. Charlie hadn't even gotten a good look at the man.

He ducked back inside and eyed the gift table. The man had been loitering there. It stood to reason that— there! Something was missing! Charlie looked closer. There had been a small blue box sitting on the corner of the table. He vaguely remembered seeing it earlier. Not overly heavy. Had barely left an imprint, but it had been slightly damp on one corner, and a trace of the blue had stained the cloth beneath. Easy enough to slip into a pocket, certainly.

The thief probably knew what was inside. The table hadn't been rifled through. Someone had deliberately picked that package. Charlie ran calculations for probable weight and size in his head and lined that up with likely valuable contents. Jewellery. Given modern fashion sense, that meant the bride.

He sighed to himself and snuck away to the adjoining chambers. The bride was a Lady Annette…

something. He couldn't remember. She was marrying Sterling's son and it was quite the event. He would have struggled to care less, but at least someone had kindly tried to make the day interesting for him. Unfortunately, his questioning didn't go well. The first problem arose because he forgot to knock. His mind was fixated on the problem at hand as he strode into the bride's chambers.

She was sitting on a side cabinet with her skirts hauled up, her legs in the air, and the only bridesmaid in the room kneeling with her head between her thighs. Sounds of passion quickly turned into screams of alarm as Charlie appeared in the open doorway.

"Apologies for the intrusion, I just need to speak with you about a theft," he said, waving them both down. "You can keep going," he instructed the bridesmaid. "I just need to talk to Annette."

"GET OUT!" the bride shrieked at him.

"Blue box, about this big," he motioned.

More screaming started behind him. Charlie was shoved into the doorframe as Lady Sterling barged into the room.

"I knew it!" the old lady cried. "You unfaithful bitch! You adulterous harlot!"

"Ladies, please!" Charlie implored. "Blue box, this big, rather generic man, brunette, pale but ruddy complexion, high forehead—"

No one was listening to him. All the women were screaming bloody murder at each other. Annette was accusing Sterling of being a meddlesome arrogant bitch who set a detective on her. Sterling was elaborating on her previous insults and praising Shilling for uncovering the infidelity. He didn't care about the sex at all, not that he could explain that. His every attempt to interject was met with louder shrieking and arguing. At the point where he had to dodge a slap, he decided his interrogation would have to wait.

"If anyone changes their mind, a commonplace thief stole a small blue box!" he called out as he ducked from the room, shutting the door safely behind him. No one followed. The screaming was still piercing, even muffled by the door. Charlie sighed to himself and wandered back through to the entranceway.

Servants were coming through into a separate hall with trays of food for after the ceremony. Charlie watched a tray of small cucumber sandwiches go by, and then he pinched two, given that no one here seemed to care about thievery. He wandered back into the main hall of the church, quietly munching his sandwiches. Footsteps descended around him almost instantly. He recognised the stride of his sisters.

"Charlie!" Rebecca hissed. "What on earth do you think you are doing?!"

"Ruminating," he answered simply, back to staring at the windows as he took another bite of sandwich.

"Where did you get the sandwiches?" Susan asked in a deadly quiet voice.

"Servants," he answered.

"You cannot just start eating the catering!" Rebecca hissed. "That food is for after the wedding."

"Honestly, Becky, I'm not really sure there will be a wedding, and it would be wrong to waste good food,"

Charlie sighed, taking another bite of sandwich. "There was a thief and an affair and now there's a room full of people yelling at each other." He sighed a muffled sandwich sigh and grimaced. "Weddings are so tedious."

It took another two hours for the wedding to be officially called off, and Charlie managed to steal a significant number of sandwiches in that time. At least he wasn't hungry on the trip home. His sisters didn't say a word to him the entire way, which was also quite nice. Although, he wasn't wholly sure what he'd done to deserve it.

Once he was home, he went straight to his room to record everything he could remember about the crime he had witnessed, complete with a rough sketch of the culprit. He was so absorbed in his work he didn't notice the knock at the front door or the voices conversing downstairs. He barely noticed the knock on his own door. He heard it; it just didn't seem to register.

"Bad time, Sleuth?" a teasing voice queried.

Charlie turned sharply. A very handsome, well-dressed man with long dark curls was standing in his doorway grinning at him.

"Swift!" Charlie jumped up. "What are you doing here?"

He moved to embrace his friend and Julian caught him with a warm familiarity, kissing his cheek.

"I was hoping to catch you in some post-wedding inebriation and have you tell me all your darkest secrets," Julian teased, "but it sounds like you've foiled that plan."

"Everyone's acting like I did something," Charlie huffed. "I wasn't the one with my head between the bride's legs."

Julian grinned at him. "I think I'm going to need the rest of that story…" He shrugged out of his overcoat and tossed it casually across the end of Charlie's bed, before flopping elegantly into the only uncluttered armchair available. His expression was expectant.

"There isn't much more to that story," Charlie sighed, but he ran through the basics anyway and showed Julian his notes.

"Hm," Julian mused. "So, you're set to be armpit deep in the case of the little blue box for a while?"

"I'm not sure," Charlie replied, setting his notes back on his desk and measuring Julian's expression and tone. "I'm intrigued, to be sure. You sound like you have a job for me?"

"I have a business proposition for you," Julian stated, settling comfortably in the chair. He motioned to all the pottery on the mantlepiece and scattered about the room. "I want to rent part of your studio. I've negotiated with Huxley for use of her kiln, and I've hired a small shop down the road."

"You're doing it?" Charlie beamed. "You're finally starting your business?"

"I'm hoping to," Julian nodded.

"You're welcome to share the studio," Charlie

smiled. "Do you still want to sell some of this junk?"

"It's not junk, Sleuth," Julian grinned at him. "If you want to get rid of some of it, I would be happy to run it through the store for you, for a small commission."

Charlie opened his mouth.

"Don't say 'keep the profit'!" Julian cut him off. "You believe in artists getting paid for their work, Charlie. Don't diminish that rule just because you don't think your work is worth anything."

"It's just the stuff I make when I'm thinking," Charlie shrugged.

"The why doesn't matter," Julian assured. "What's important is that you made it. If you don't want the money, you can donate it, I don't care. I want this shop. I want to do something honest with my life. I want to create things. As my friend, I want to offer you the chance to be a part of that too. I know you're too busy to do anything like this yourself, but you make wonderful pieces that you then store badly until you throw tantrums and break them. I'm offering an alternative that might even help fund some of your other exploits."

"Help yourself to whatever you like," Charlie shrugged. "If it has my mark on it, it's yours. I want you to succeed at this, Swift, whatever that may look like for you."

"You're a good friend, Charlie," Julian thanked him, unfolding from the chair and embracing him again. Charlie snuggled into the hug. Like everything in his life, physical interactions were an all-or-nothing event. He didn't like being touched by strangers. He liked being hugged by Julian. Julian was tall and strong and he smelled good. Charlie had never had a big brother, but Julian was exactly what he imagined that would be like.

"You're a good friend too, Swift," he replied.

"Tell Bronny that," Julian grimaced, letting him go. "She's not best pleased with me at the moment. She makes out it's because I'm leaving, but we both knew I was just passing through. I think she knows I told Lizzie that there was an option to make a little extra on the side."

"You invited Lizzie to run for Michael?" Charlie raised an eyebrow.

Julian shrugged. "Just from the House. She's the right kind of discreet, so she'd be good at it. I like to think it would be good for her. You know she's been so apprehensive and insecure since the attack. I just want her to know there are options."

"I'm sure she does know," Charlie replied. "She's been balancing her recovery very well, or so I hear."

"She broke things off with Doctor Florin this morning..." Julian told him, folding elegantly back into the chair.

Charlie froze. His brain whirred as he processed this. That meant that Florin had just been heartlessly discarded before Lionel found her... just before Charlie had lied to her. No wonder she had looked so tight around the eyes. The anger wasn't wholly because of the gossipmongering reporters, although they were a good place to direct it. Dear God, he needed to apologise. Perhaps he should write her a letter... then he could practice the words —

"Penny for your thoughts, Sleuth?" Julian smiled at him.

"No," Charlie replied.

Julian chuckled. There was a warmth in his dark eyes as mirth crinkled his face. Charlie could feel his friend watching him knowingly and refused to feed that fire. Besides, it wasn't like Swift was above his own worthy pursuits of mockery.

"This shop…" Charlie began.

"Mm?" Julian queried.

"You'll have to stop running for Michael entirely," Charlie mused. "Between crafting and selling, you're not going to have time for espionage as well. What are you going to do?"

"Quit," Julian admitted.

"You've already told him?" Charlie deduced. "How did he take it?"

"Fine," Julian shrugged casually. "He was very polite about it. You know our Skipp."

Charlie sighed tragically and perched on the arm of a nearby chair. He propped himself up like a renaissance figure lamenting what could have been.

"You should have swooped in dramatically and kissed him," he muttered. "Proper Shakespearian spectacle, real *Knights of Tintagel* type ordeal."

Julian refrained from replying, or laughing, instead turning his face to the window. The lace curtains were drawn, but the street and the bakery were still visible through the sheer fabric. Charlie watched his expression, pulling truths from the details. He perked up slowly.

"Oh… you did…" he smirked.

Julian turned to him sharply. Charlie was leaning towards him over his crossed knees, unable to wipe the widening grin from his face. Julian rolled his eyes. Charlie cackled.

"Shut up," Julian huffed, more to silence his expression than his voice.

"I can't," Charlie preened. "I'm too busy being smug."

Julian leapt up from the chair and Charlie dashed away as the bigger man tried to grab him. He laughed as Julian chased him around the room, yelling at him. Charlie bounced over the bed and swore he felt Julian's fingers nearly snag the back of his shirt. He stumbled and turned. They faced each other across the mattress, both trying to discern which way the other would go.

"I'm really not the person you should be chasing around the bed," Charlie teased.

Julian snatched a pillow from the bed and threw it at Charlie, smacking him in the face with it.

"Hey!" A second pillow whacked him. "No! Stop! We have to put them back or the maids will try and clean!"

"Ah," Julian smirked, grabbing the bedsheets and hauling them back into an unkempt mess. "It's all fun and games until someone involves an oppressive class system, aye?"

"Julian! Put the sheets back!" Charlie yelled.

They both froze as footsteps sounded in the doorway. Rebecca stood watching them with one eyebrow raised.

"This isn't what it looks like," Julian tried to assure her.

"I had no intention of asking, Mister Silver," she replied. "Could you please convince him to let someone clean the room? It looks like a cannon went off in here."

"No! Stay out!" Charlie hissed like a rabid ferret. "Everything is where I need it to be."

"You live like an animal, Charlie," Rebecca protested, motioning to the clutter.

He felt that was hyperbolic enough to be considered an outright lie, and he really didn't see the problem with his sprawling collections. They inspired the mind and radicalised thoughts in a way minimalism could never hope to achieve. It helped to remember things if they were in plain sight, laid out in a careful order, each piece a specifically designed carriage in an artificially constructed train of thought.

"An animal in the bedroom anyway," Julian teased.

Charlie threw one of the pillows violently back at him. Julian managed to catch it with his hands rather than his face, looking awfully smug.

"That sounds like your business, not mine," Rebecca commented. "But perhaps close the door."

"It's really not what you think it is!" Julian called after her as she walked away and left them to their shenanigans.

"She's teasing you," Charlie sighed, picking up the other pillow and straightening it on the bed, before pulling the bedsheets neatly back into place. "She teases with a very straight face, but she knows we don't have that kind of relationship."

"Does she now?" Julian smirked. "And why is that? Is there something about you she does know? Involving anyone in particular perhaps…?" He moved the pillow back and forth in his hands teasingly and then paused, moving it closer to his face and sniffing. "Is that Florin's perfume?"

Charlie felt his stomach drop and his face flush.

"Sleuth, tell me you washed the pillowcase in the last two months!" Julian exclaimed.

"Of course I washed the pillow!" Charlie huffed, so stained with embarrassment he didn't realise he'd made it worse until it was too late.

"So you actively bought the same perfume and reapplied it?" Julian deduced.

Charlie had never wanted to dive out the window so badly in his life. He felt like he was about to catch fire. Somehow, it felt worse than the last time he'd been in an actual burning room. This metaphorical fire was so much more personal.

"It smells nice…" he whispered in a tiny and utterly mortified voice.

"Charlie!" Julian laughed at him.

"It's soothing…" His voice got smaller.

Julian was laughing so hard he nearly doubled over. Charlie was so deeply entrenched in the flames of embarrassment that he was near death. He had worried the behaviour was disturbing, that perhaps he was troubled, but he hoped that troubled people didn't worry about such things. Besides, he'd been looking into it, there were legitimate herbal reasons that the scent was soothing and helped him sleep. Not that he was going to try and use that defence with Julian, who would undoubtedly still find a way to make it about Florin.

"Don't make me beat you with that pillow," Charlie grumbled.

Julian laughed harder. Charlie pulled a face. He knew his sisters referred to him as a scruffy little twig boy, and they were probably not alone in their description. He won less than half the fights he engaged in, and the victories usually only occurred because he fought dirty. Julian still occasionally tried to treat him like he was recovering from his stabbing, even though it had been months ago. Right now, he'd probably just try and take advantage of it. Julian tossed the pillow gently back into place on the bed.

"You're hopeless, Charlie..." he grinned affectionately. "We both know I can take you, but I don't really want to explain the bite marks to Mike."

"I won't bite," Charlie promised.

"I know you, Sleuth," Julian laughed. "You're a biter. You can't help yourself."

"Gotta do something when you're the smallest," Charlie shrugged, rubbing his crooked nose.

"Come on," Julian motioned to him. He picked up his coat from the end of the bed and draped an arm around Charlie's shoulders as he neared. "I want to show you the shop, and then you can buy me a drink and we can discuss the studio."

"You can just use it," Charlie shrugged. "I don't care."

"That's why you're buying drinks," Julian sighed. "Because I'm going to have to negotiate on behalf of both of us."

4

The next day was clear and bright and splendid. The sunlight sparkled through stained glass windows and lit the tearoom brightly from the open front doors. It had about it that sharp mid-morning quality that reflected off everything it touched with a harsh glow.

Amy relaxed back in her chair, basking in the warmth. She sipped at her tea and listened fondly to Jane and Laura as they discussed the work they had been involved with since graduation. Laura was looking into further post-graduate research with the university and Jane had joined a private practice. It was exciting times, but she was still waiting for either of them to bring up the new rings they were sporting.

"Some of the house calls have been rather nightmarish," Jane admitted. "But I think I lucked out with the practice overall. Doctor Maine has been ever so supportive."

"Yes, she's very encouraging when it comes to new graduates," Laura agreed. "I quite like her. I'm sure you could talk to her about work, Amy, when you're ready, of course. Jane and I can put in a good word for you too if you want. She's very easy to chat to."

Amy smiled. She was fairly confident that Laura

found absolutely anyone easy to talk to. It was one of her most endearing features, coupled with the fact that she was easy to talk to herself. Laura was one of those people you could tell anything to and she would listen and support you no matter what. Jane was much the same.

Amy was trying so hard not to... what had Lizzie called it? Do a Charlie. She was railing against it like a storm. It shouldn't be hard to simply sit here and enjoy tea and cake with friends. Except she could see how hard they were trying to include her in their endeavours, and they would not tell her about the rings. It almost seemed as though they were trying to draw attention away from them. There was an eager desperation about them, like they were trying to make her happy. They didn't need to try. She was happy just to be with them.

"I do have a question..." she raised, gently setting her teacup down.

"Mm?" Laura perked up.

Unable to help herself, she gave both of them and their rings a direct look. They caught on and their expressions became bashful and apologetic.

"So that's a thing..." Laura admitted.

"You were always observant..." Jane conceded.

"I take it you two are engaged?" she smiled at them. "When did it happen and how come you didn't tell me?"

"Oh, it's quite recent!" Laura assured.

"We decided we wanted to get formally engaged after graduation," Jane elaborated. "As for telling you about it…" she trailed off.

"We didn't want to upset you," Laura filled in. "It seemed cruel to flaunt our engagement when yours… uh…"

"Imploded?" Amy offered. "Horrifically and publicly."

"Quite," Jane agreed sympathetically. "You know there's absolutely no judgement from us, but you never talk about Harry, so…"

"We don't want to bring it up if you don't," Laura finished Jane's sentence again.

Amy smiled at them. She reached across the table, taking each of their hands in one of hers and squeezing their fingers lovingly.

"Thank you," she smiled. "I appreciate it, I really do, but I don't need that much coddling. I want good news in my life. I want your good news! I'm happy for you both, truly! I couldn't be more pleased." She realised she was gushing, but they seemed as genuinely pleased as she was.

"Well, in that case…" Laura began and proceeded to rattle off the tale of Jane proposing to her in the rose garden during one of their afternoon walks. Amy sat back again and grinned at them, happy to sip her tea and be lost in the atmosphere and romance of it all.

"I have a question for you too," Jane raised as Laura finished her story.

"Oh yes?" Amy lifted her eyebrows curiously.

"Have you spoken to either of them yet?" Jane asked.

Amy pursed her lips sourly and her mood plummeted. She wanted to accuse them of conspiring with Lizzie, but she knew they hadn't. They were checking in on her. It was kind. It just didn't feel that way. She had told everyone who had asked that she wasn't going to speak to Harry for the rest of her life. She threw all his letters unopened into the fire and ignored all requests that she visit. She wouldn't. Seeing him at the trial was already more than she wanted.

Shilling was another matter entirely. She didn't like the way Charlie and Harry got lumped together. She knew why they did — the detective and the murderer — it made perfect sense. The two people whose actions had brought her life and family crashing to their knees. But Charlie hadn't killed anyone — hadn't hurt anyone, at least, not intentionally. He had just been doing his job. She told herself that every day. There was no reason to see him again. The case was over. Everyone was moving on.

"Actually, I did see Mister Shilling yesterday morning…" she admitted, pouring another cup of tea from the pot and stirring a lump of sugar into it.

Laura and Jane both leant forward conspiratorially. Amy shot their indiscretion a dour look.

"Really?" she huffed.

"Yes, really," Laura replied unabashedly. "It's good that you finally saw him!"

Jane raised a neat hand to pause her fiancée before they got ahead of themselves. "Did you speak to him?" she pressed.

"Why do you care?" Amy sighed. "Seriously, the man was just doing his job."

"But you did kiss him…" Laura reminded.

"As part of a trap to bait Harry," Amy snapped, loathing the hot blush that rose in her cheeks.

"Did you speak to him?" Jane repeated.

"Yes!" Amy snapped. "Yes, all right, fine. We spoke. Briefly. It was just in passing on the street."

"So, you didn't actually go and see him?" Laura rebuked.

"I never said I did," Amy glowered. "I said I saw him. I was returning home when I was accosted by one of those awful photographers outside the front gate. Shilling happened to be there and he stepped in."

They stared at her.

"Tell us everything," Laura insisted, reaching across the table to pat her hand.

Amy rolled her eyes, but caved. She considered playing down his actions to avoid sparking her friends' inclination to romanticise the rescue, but decided to stick to honesty. Besides, it wasn't like Charlie was chivalrous on purpose. He was righteous and ferociously honourable, which sometimes masqueraded as chivalry, but his lie would speak for itself. She was recounting his timid mutterings about Lady Sterling when Laura and Jane gave her 'the look'. Amy paused mid-tale to glance around. She started as the old lady herself appeared right at her shoulder.

"Oh dearie, I didn't mean to spook you," Lady Sterling patted her arm.

"Apologies, Ma'am," Amy gasped, resting a hand on her bodice. "I didn't realise you were there."

"I don't mean to interrupt you ladies, but I couldn't help but overhear," Sterling began curiously. "You're

Doctor Amelia Florin, aren't you? Lord Pound's little girl?"

Amy nodded slowly, unsure what she was getting herself into.

"You work with Charles Shilling, yes?" Sterling assumed.

"No, I—" Amy stammered.

"You helped him catch the Jack, didn't you?" the old lady pressed.

Amy felt her mouth dry up and her tongue start to stick. She didn't know what to say. Sterling leant in closer.

"You tell him thank you for his help at the wedding, and I am keen to speak to him about the missing *'pearls'*." She put a suspicious lean on the word that made Amy stare at her.

"I'm sorry, the what?" she murmured.

"The *'pearls'*," Sterling repeated slyly. "The missing box of diamonds he's been hunting down for me. Very clever codeword you two must've come up with. Nice and discreet. Anyway, after the nightmare of yesterday, I didn't have time to talk to him, but you tell him to let me know how it's going. He can name his price." Sterling patted her arm again. "I don't know how you do it, love. You must be as patient as Susan and Rebecca to put up with that odd duck, but he does have his uses, doesn't he?"

"He does..." Amy admitted slowly.

"Odd duck though," Sterling repeated.

"The oddest duck..." Amy agreed. Half of her wanted to send the old lady away and tell anyone listening that she was not Shilling's messenger girl, but she was far too curious. Also… he hadn't been lying. She'd dismissed him unfairly when, of course, he'd been telling the truth. She knew he didn't lie. She'd known it was odd, but she'd been too self-absorbed to consider the alternatives.

Sterling gave her a knowing smile and moved away. Amy looked back at her friends. Their expressions made her roll her eyes and despair.

"Oh shut up," she huffed at them.

"Didn't say a word…" Jane smiled, sipping her tea.

"But we can drop you off on the way back," Laura grinned, scooping a dainty forkful of cake.

Charlie couldn't believe how often he forgot the simplest of things. It was like his brain just didn't work properly. There were things he knew, and things he knew he knew, and somehow he still forgot them. His plans for breakfast had involved rising early to scale a building for some light B&E and minor scandal. However, in the process of breaking and entering, he fell through the unlocked window, forgetting that Michael's windows opened inward. Most importantly, he had forgotten that bakers rose well before the dawn.

He crashed face first onto the wooden floor and groaned. The windows swung listlessly in the first rays of golden light. Most of the room was obscured from view behind the desk he had fallen behind. It was a simple room with scant furniture. The most impressive things were the desk and storage cupboards. Although, the bed had been upgraded. The figure in it leapt up, but paused at the pitiful sound of Charlie groaning.

"Sleuth? Is that you?" Julian strode over completely naked and helped pull him off the floor.

"I leant on the window to get my lockpicks out…" Charlie muttered, rubbing his head.

"Wasn't locked, mate," Julian told him.

"I'm aware," Charlie sighed.

"Shutters open out. Windows open in," Julian told him.

"I'm aware," Charlie groaned.

"Mike's already downstairs. Ya coulda just knocked on the door." Julian stifled a yawn and his natural accent nearly crept in for a moment. Charlie glowered and Julian cracked a grin. "But I guess you knew that too, aye?"

The door burst open. Mike rushed into the room with an iron skillet raised in one hand. He paused as soon as he saw them and gave them both a quizzical look.

"Charlie…?" He managed to make the 'what are you doing here?' implicit in his tone.

"Fell through the window," Julian offered helpfully, patting Charlie on the back. "Forgot windows open in."

Mike lowered the skillet but his confusion didn't soften in the slightest. Charlie could see the question 'what were you doing at my window?' sitting neatly across his face.

"I was looking for Swift," Charlie nodded his head

at Julian.

"Congratulations," Michael commented drily, motioning to the naked man in implication of Charlie finding him.

"I feel that's what I should be saying to you," Charlie grinned.

Julian completely failed to stifle his laughter and Michael went bright pink. His posture immediately became hesitant, defensive. Julian turned away from them, trying to hide his chortling as he sat back down on the side of the unmade bed. Michael couldn't seem to take his eyes off him.

"You could at least put on a robe or something…" Mike suggested, his eyes scouring Julian's naked body even as he said it.

"It's not that cold," Julian shrugged, lounging on the bed. "I thought you liked me naked?"

"He does," Charlie grinned.

Michael went, if possible, redder. Outside the door, footsteps approached on the stairs.

"Is Julian naked?" one of Mike's brothers called, trying to storm the room.

Michael grabbed his older brother by the face as he came through the doorway and shoved him forcibly from the space. There was the crash of two people hitting the stairs and one of them falling.

"What in God's name is going on up there?!" That was Terry, the oldest Pence.

Michael scampered back into his room, skillet still in hand, and didn't quite cower. Now the footsteps were heavy stomps. Terry appeared as a formidable looming presence in the doorway. He wasn't the tallest of the six Pence siblings, but he was the biggest and the loudest. He gave the room a serious raised eyebrow.

"Do I want to know?" he asked.

"The furniture in this house is creaky, I imagine you already do," Charlie replied, perching on the edge of Michael's desk and leafing through some of the notes on it. He missed the wry looks everyone else threw his way.

"I didn't realise you were involved, Sleuth," Terry commented pointedly.

"Oh, I'm not," Charlie looked up from the notes. "I'm just being nosy."

"Well, at least someone's allowed to be!" a voice called up the stairs.

"You all right, John?" Terry yelled down. "Any injuries?"

"Just my pride," John called back. "You'd think Mike would be in a better mood for jokes this morning after the night he had!"

"He's just tired," Terry shouted back with a wolfish smirk.

Michael glowered at his brother venomously. Terry's grin widened.

"I hate all of you," Mike muttered.

"We hate you more," Terry told him lovingly, patting his back. "Maybe see how much of the business you can keep upstairs today. I don't mind you running it through the bakery as long as it doesn't hamper our work."

"I'll be back downstairs as soon as Sleuth's done

robbing us," Michael replied, eyeballing Charlie who was back to digging through his papers.

"He's an anarchist, Mikey, not a thief," Terry grinned. "Boy only knows how to work, eh Sleuth? Solving the case of how my neurotic, smart-arse brother caught himself such a sickeningly handsome boyfriend?"

"The only question I have in that regard is why it took them so long," Charlie replied without looking up. He was only half paying attention to the conversation now. The notes were interesting.

"Oh dear... I know that face," Julian commented, watching him. He stood and began to dress as though Charlie's interest in the paperwork would have something to do with him. Charlie scanned the notes again and pulled a face. He could see why Julian might think that. There was more than one piece of fascinating news scrawled in Michael's collection.

"Have you seen this?" he asked, handing over the sheet of paper once Julian finished buttoning his trousers.

Julian took the notes and scanned them, starting at the top and beginning to frown.

"Duke Sovereign is coming down from Edinburgh to visit with the Queen..." he read.

"He hasn't been south over the border since he killed his son," Terry commented.

"Since he what?" Mike turned to him.

"Oh come on," Terry scoffed. "The man's only son and heir suddenly goes missing and the old bastard doesn't even bother looking for him? It doesn't take our mate Shilling here to figure that one out."

"The Duke didn't kill his son," Shilling replied.

Terry rolled his eyes. "Here I was wondering if the old man was coming to hire you, and it sounds like you've already cracked the case."

"He won't hire me, he's not looking for his son, he's not going to start looking, and even if he did, I wouldn't tell him anything," Charlie sighed. "Rory and his father hate each other with a passion rivalling Zeus and Kronos. It's easier to keep them both alive if they're never in the same room together. That's not what we're looking at." He motioned to Julian to keep reading.

Julian's frown deepened with disgust.

"A group of Harry Pound's peers are trying to petition for his release?" he exclaimed in disbelief. "They claim that he was provoked and that his actions were a necessary evil that—!" Julian choked in outrage. "Where do you find this garbage, Skipp?!"

"It's true," Mike assured him bleakly. "A group of Harry's friends are trying to petition on his behalf. Wealthy socialites from the clubs he belonged to who think they should be above the law."

"I call them LOAM," Charlie announced.

"Because they're as low as dirt?" Julian construed.

"Not entirely, but I love how you think, Swift," Charlie smiled. "It stands for League Of Aristocratic Misogynists. They won't get anywhere. Too many of the women who were killed come from high-born families. They're just vile, entitled, loathsome men who admire Pound Junior and the violent power fetish he embodies for them. No court will hear them out, and they're not arguing he didn't do it."

"Good God, Charlie," Julian grinned at him. "I wish I could say 'aristocratic' with half the venom you do."

"Number six," Charlie sighed at him, motioning him to continue down the list. They were getting distracted from the important things.

"The Sterling and Merrill wedding…?" Julian began, glancing up from the paper. "Which our Sleuth here so publicly axed yesterday—"

"I was not the one who—" Charlie erupted.

"Aye, aye, Charlie," Julian grinned, flicking the paper up. "We know. Would that you were though… that would make quite the story."

"You first," he countered.

"I'm spoken for," Julian replied smugly, laying a hand over his breast before continuing with the notes. "It says here that three days before the wedding, Annette Merrill had someone called Philippe Balles added to the guest list…"

"For the ceremony but not the reception," Charlie added keenly.

"I thought you said you found her with a bridesmaid?" Julian cocked an eyebrow.

"I did — this is not about the affair!" Charlie huffed. "God, why does everyone care about the wedding?!"

"Because we're normal, Charlie," Mike told him.

"And it's funny," Terry added.

Charlie snatched the paper from Julian's hand and waved it at them.

"Philippe Balles was invited to the wedding last minute by the bride, he is a known associate of Lucille

Bonheur, which makes me wonder where the connection between Merrill and Bonheur occurs."

"No one else knows who Lucille Bonheur is, Charlie," Michael sighed.

Charlie paused and considered the room. That was probably true, and his friends only ever seemed to lie to him if they were lying to themselves as well. Odds were this was out of their depth, even for their chief intelligence gatherer. He set the notes neatly back in their stack and pulled a careful face.

"Lucille Bonheur is a woman who goes by many names," he explained.

There were several noises of comprehension. They all knew what that meant.

"And one of her people stole something from the wedding?" Julian asked.

"Possibly not…" Charlie replied. He saw Julian roll his eyes and knew he'd lost him.

"But you said—"

"I know! I know, I thought so too," Charlie appeased him. "However, given that Merrill knew Balles was coming and added him to the guest list, it is possible that it wasn't thievery at all, but intended to be a discreet transaction. It is possible the parcel was left there for Balles to collect. But then where is the connection between Merrill and Bonheur and why was the bride paying off another woman on her wedding day…?"

"I can think of three immediate reasons," Julian quipped, buttoning his waistcoat.

"We know what you're thinking, Swift," Michael

smirked at him. "I can look into it if you want, Sleuth? My people can poke around."

"You know it could just be their business?" Terry suggested pointedly.

The other three men paused mid-action and turned to him in unison.

"Other people's business is our business, Terry," Julian grinned, swinging his long black coat on with characteristic flare. Terry rolled his eyes disdainfully and turned from the room, trudging back downstairs to escape the vanity. Charlie was eyeing Julian's attire. Swift was dressing to leave.

"Any chance you could get me in to see Lady Merrill this morning, Swift?" he asked.

Julian laughed. "After the stunt you pulled yesterday, Sleuth? Not a hope in Hell." He flicked his collar up and clamped an arm around Charlie's shoulders. "Come on, I still need to borrow you before you try and make every shady deal in London your next case." He dragged him towards the doorway.

"Do you think there might be bread...?" Charlie inquired hopefully.

"Why don't you go ask?" Julian encouraged, ushering him towards the stairs. "They like you."

The other Pence siblings were inferred but Charlie paused in the doorway. It took him altogether too long to realise that he was being dismissed and why. Julian descended on Mike like a wolf cornering a rabbit. Although Charlie would be the first to admit his analogy might include a suicidal rabbit. Julian tangled his fingers in Michael's dark blonde hair, pressing him to the wall as he kissed him. Michael seemed to melt in his hands, surrendering helplessly as the skillet slipped from his fingers and hit the floor with a bang. He held Julian delicately, like he was worried he'd disappear.

Charlie watched for a moment, but comfortably convinced his friends were getting along as well as he could hope, he quickly grew bored and left. They didn't need an audience, he'd rather not watch, Julian would know where to find him when he was ready, and — most importantly — there would be fresh bread downstairs.

5

Amy had seriously considered not getting herself involved. The problem then lay in her overwhelming personal curiosity and her friends' Machiavellian ability to meddle. Not to mention the filthy secret she was forced to admit to herself as she stood on Lady Guinea's doorstep: she did actually want to see him again. He was easy company, and he made her think harder and feel smarter. Not bad qualities in a friend. If he was interested in being friends.

Jane and Laura had dropped her at Guinea's house, so the only thing left was to knock. There was no point running away. Besides, she had Sterling's excuse for being there. The door was opened by Jasper, who gave her a cool once-over with his eyes and smiled haughtily.

"Doctor Florin, a pleasant surprise, my Lady. We weren't expecting you," he greeted her.

"Is Ch—" she cleared her throat. "Is Mister Shilling in?"

Jasper's smile evolved into something truly wicked, and she regretted asking.

"He's in the studio with Master Silver," the butler replied.

"If he's busy I can come back another time," she tried

to brush away casually, panicking internally.

"Not at all," Jasper insisted, standing aside and motioning for her to enter. "Master Shilling would be furious if I told him he'd missed you. Please, let me show you to the studio."

With no excuse to back out, she stepped inside and followed Jasper down the corridor towards the back of the house. She could hear Julian laughing before they entered and wondered for a moment what she was getting herself into. Jasper led her into a room that was surprisingly spacious and light, with large windows overlooking the picturesque garden out the back.

"Gentlemen, may I present Doctor Florin," Jasper introduced. It wore the guise of a question but it most certainly was not.

Florin stood in the doorway, hands clasped politely in front of her skirt, and braced herself. The space was being used as a pottery studio. There were old sheets across the floor, with pottery wheels and glazing and painting stations set up around the room. Julian sat at the nearest wheel. His clothes were far more raggedy than usual, with his sleeves rolled up to his elbows, an apron around his waist, and his hair tied back. A few loose curls had escaped alluringly around his face.

Charlie was at the wheel further down the room. He wore loose linen trousers tied at his waist but his feet and torso were bare. Amy could see the dark scar on his ribs where he'd been stabbed two months ago. There were some old yellowing bruises spotted over his arms and body that suggested he'd gotten into something in the last few weeks. Not surprising at all. He was up to his wrists in clay and there were small smears and flecks of it across his face and chest.

"Florin?" Charlie barely glanced her way, almost incapable of taking his eyes from his work, but he did the head tilt, like a retriever convinced the ball hadn't actually been thrown.

"Fancy seeing you here, Amelia," Julian smirked at her, looking up properly.

"Hello Julian," she sighed, meeting his eye in an effort not to look at Charlie and losing the war with her blush. "I'm sorry for the intrusion. If you're busy, I can come back."

"I'm busy but you can stay," Charlie replied automatically. "I can listen while I work and can make myself available to you in five to ten minutes, if you can spare them. I just have to finish this."

He still didn't look up, but she seemed to be making up for his disinterest by staring. He was so matter of fact and so… simple. Everyone else she knew felt steeped to their hips in drama by comparison. Charlie didn't have time for that. He wasn't going to bemoan impropriety. Both these men had lived in High Houses, they probably had no idea what impropriety was. Besides, she was a doctor for God's sake! This was very far from the first half-dressed man she'd seen.

Still, she suddenly felt like the last two months had vanished, and Charlie had dragged her into Bronny's house again. She frequented the place now. She had no qualms about it. But it felt the same, standing in the studio, staring at him. He was surprisingly muscular. She had thought him scrawny, and he certainly looked like someone who forgot to eat on occasion, but the physical activity required by his sleuthing seemed to be doing him some favours. She instantly wished she hadn't thought it. Her cheeks were so hot.

"You can make yourself available to her, can you, Sleuth?" Julian teased.

Amy had a strong urge to jump in an icy river before she combusted. Charlie finally looked up from his work to glare viciously at Julian.

"Would you like me to repeat that to Skipp?" he threatened.

"Are you kidding?" Julian chuckled. "I'll tell him myself. He'll be proud of that one."

From the doorway, Jasper gave Amy a smirk that welcomed her to the menagerie and took no responsibility for whatever was about to occur, before slinking back into the shadows. She realised she must have even more in common with Shilling than everyone kept implying, including taste in friends. Laura and Jane would have approved of Julian's jest as well. They would be loving this situation and she wasn't altogether sure she was ever going to tell them about it.

There were so many safe places to look, and she couldn't drag her eyes to a single one of them. When she finally managed to look back to Julian, he was watching her with a twinkle so scandalous and smug she wanted to drag him to an open sewer by his perfect, luscious hair and drop him in.

"Admiring the view, Amelia?" he grinned.

"The gardens are lovely," she replied evenly.

"Yes, Susan is very particular about them," Charlie

contributed, keenly back to work. His hands moved so gently over the clay, shaping it delicately as it spun in his fingers. "She has someone come and tend to them. Insists on well-trimmed bushes." He paused to throw another scathing look at Julian, who was choking.

"Just laugh, Mister Silver," Amy advised drily. "Before you asphyxiate."

Julian tried to keep his laughter silent, but he was wiping at his eyes with his forearms. At least it got him off her case. Speaking of which, it would be foolish not to make the most of the moment to roll out a new distraction.

"Actually, Charlie, I'm here about a case," she announced.

"Yours or mine?" he asked.

She smiled at him helplessly. "Yours, Charlie. I don't take cases."

"You should," he replied like it was the most normal suggestion in the world.

"I'm here about your Sterling case," Amy sighed. "Regarding her 'pearls' you told me about yesterday."

Charlie's foot slowed and the wheel came to a stop. He looked up at her, suddenly flushed and awkward.

"Yes..." he muttered. "Yes... sorry about that..."

"You have nothing to be sorry for," she told him. "I'm the one who should be sorry. I was having a bad morning and I was short with you, even after you helped me. The code just... it made me think you were lying... I should know you better than that. I'm sorry—"

"No, I'm sorry, Florin," Charlie insisted, leaving his

pottery and standing imploringly. "I was lying. I did lie. I shouldn't have. I… I was just so flustered…"

"But… but the diamonds?" she checked.

"The what now?" Julian demanded.

"Sterling's diamonds…" she answered slowly. "The missing diamonds she's getting you to look for…?"

Amy couldn't take her eyes off Charlie, but at least now it was because she could see his brain whirring at speed. His brows creased seriously over his grey eyes as he played catch up in record time. His gaze dropped to his muddy hands.

"Wash," he muttered like an order to himself. He quickly sat back at the wheel, took his clay cutter, and slid it under the base of the vase he had shaped. With delicate precision, he cut the piece free and set it with half a dozen others on a tray waiting to be fired. He set his tools aside and stood again. Focused and meticulous. His gaze flicked back up and he met Amy's eye with sharp ruthlessness. "Tell me everything, Florin."

She made to open her mouth, but he had already turned away. He strode across the room to the basin at the side, turning the tap with his elbow and rinsing his hands in the water. The drops hit the bottom of the metal basin loudly as she began to speak.

"Closer, Florin," Charlie bid her, motioning her nearer. "I can't hear."

Her heart and her temperature felt like they were rising with every step she took as she approached him. She tried to keep a polite distance, but it was difficult with the noise. Julian's gaze was like a hovering dagger between her shoulders. She stood too close to see anything but Charlie as he rinsed his taut, pale arms in the cold water.

She carefully ran him through the morning's affair at the teahouse, and Sterling's assumptions and confessions, including her invitation to bring Charlie to see her. Charlie leant over the sink and splashed water across his face and body, rinsing himself off. Amy nearly choked. She wished she could look away from the subtle droplets trickling across his skin. She wished it wasn't causing her to flush and suffocate like her corset was shrinking.

"I tried to correct her," she admitted, hating the strain in her voice. "But when I realised what must have happened, I decided it couldn't hurt to bring her message to you, as I ought to apologise anyway—"

"I cannot impress enough that you have nothing to apologise for," he insisted, turning the tap off and reaching for a nearby hand towel. He dried his hands and dabbed at his skin before turning back to her. She felt like she was about to faint from the knot in her chest, but his grey eyes were so calm and serious that when they met hers again the temperature seemed to drop until she could breathe. "Florin, we are living through a series of bizarre coincidences," he confessed. "I did lie. I had no idea what had been stolen — I was starting to think nothing had been. All I knew was that a small blue box had been taken from the gift table and I didn't learn about it until I was at the wedding that afternoon. When I saw you that morning I wasn't working. I lied. I'm sorry. I was on your street because I was coming to see you."

There it was, that woozy sensation came right back. It seemed she ought to feel elated, but she actually felt like she'd been slapped.

"What?" she replied, reeling in confusion.

"It was my fifth attempt," he continued. "In the last two months I have come by your door five times, but I have yet to knock — much to the aggravation of my friends and family."

"Here, here!" Julian called across the room.

"I wished to check in on you," Charlie ignored his friend. "I was worried for you and your father after everything that occurred with Pound Junior, and especially with everything that has been going on in the papers since. Many times I have talked myself into a visit to enquire after your health, and to offer any assistance the two of you might want amidst this mess, but I flee like a coward every time. I can't bring myself to knock. The guilt of my part in Harry's fate still outweighs the guilt of my absence in your lives. After everything that happened, I can't stop telling myself that I must be the last person either of you would ever want to see again. I was in the process of running away yesterday when you arrived, but I couldn't abandon you to be accosted by Lionel Tanner. When you asked what I was doing, all my fear erupted to the surface and I panicked. I did lie, badly. I was too flustered to admit the truth because I couldn't imagine you would want to have anything to do with me. I'm sorry, Florin. I know things have aligned so that I can pretend that wasn't the case, but somehow that makes it worse. I cannot in good conscience lie again to present myself in a more favourable light, which I certainly do not deserve — especially as it makes you believe you have something to apologise for, which you certainly do not. I must remedy the lie. I am deeply remorseful for my cowardice in the face of your distress. My selfish anxiety got the better of me and it was wrong."

Amy took a deep, slow breath. She wasn't sure if she wanted to kiss him or slap him, and neither were appropriate.

"If you need a moment to process my transgressions I should go upstairs and change anyway," he finished, wiping his damp hair from his face.

"Take her with you, Sleuth," Julian called. "You never know what sudden onsets of clarity might strike her while you're pantsless." His tone gave no room for even Charlie to misread the insinuation.

Charlie went scarlet. His expression froze at peak mortification. It was the only thing that kept Amy from doing the same. She turned to the smirking harlot.

"Mister Silver, shut your mouth before I come over there and shove it full of whatever muck you're fingering," she ordered.

Julian laughed. "As inviting as you make that sound, Amelia, I'm afraid I've left the House and gone exclusive." He grinned at her with unreserved delight. "I'm courting the boy next door."

"Courting or ploughing?" she retorted.

He laughed again, and this time his vicious mockery seemed to melt away, as though conceding he could take as good as he gave. His smile was so genuine. It creased his eyes and softened his face.

"That was fair," he surrendered. "But I love him, Amy. I really do. You should meet him. He doesn't embroil himself in Sleuth's business like we do, but he's just as tuned in with all the goings on. He is easily as quick-witted as our Charlie, but manifests it quite differently."

"This is one of the Pence siblings from the bakery?" Amy checked. "The one you call Skipp?"

"Michael Pence," Charlie agreed, finally finding his tongue again. "Skipp's short for Skipper, because, inevitably, he's the boss. Swift used to run for him, and I solve cases for him — well, for the people who hire me through him. You might have seen him if you've ever been by the bakery; ordinary bloke, about 5'9", dark blonde hair, usually dressed like he's working the bakery even though most of his business happens in the back-back room."

"How dare you!" Julian demanded. "Mike is not ordinary. He is exceptional and beautiful. He has eyes with the wisdom and colour of an ageless fountain spring, and hair like the finest drizzle of dark honey, and freckles like constellations scattered across his body. He has a smile like the glowing dawn, a wit so cuttingly sharp it bites, yet tempered by a voice so gentle and even it makes you shiver. He is all the wonders of creation bound in a single, perfect human form."

Amy froze for a moment in the wake of Julian's passionate declaration, before turning to Charlie.

"Oh, he's got it something truly chronic, doesn't he?"

she said.

Charlie met her look with eyes as big as saucers and a helpless melted droop to his posture.

"I love how in love they are," he replied weakly.

Amy resisted a chuckle. She remembered the one night she had spent in Charlie's room, traumatised by the revelation of Harry, while Charlie ignored the pending horror of the serial killer to spy out the window at his friends. Coupled with the extensive collection of erotic romance novels on his bedstand, she should not have been surprised by the reaction. If only he could show the same interest in another person as he did in matchmaking and problem solving. It was foolish to even think it.

"Go and get dressed, Charlie, we have a big afternoon ahead," she sighed at him.

"We do?" he queried.

"I rather think I should accompany you to Sterling's interview," Amy said. "She already believes us to be working together, after all, and we have proven that two heads were better than one in the past. Besides, as inspired as Mister Silver's poetry regarding his new love is, I don't think I could stand an entire afternoon with it."

"You're going so you're not seen as the messenger girl," Julian smirked.

"I'm not a messenger girl," Amy retorted.

"Go put some pants on, Sleuth," Julian encouraged. "You've got yourself a new partner in crime-solving."

"And you've got new gossip to run to Skipp," Charlie replied. "This is turning into a real case."

6

Lady Sterling's London townhouse was nearby to Susan Guinea's, so they walked. It hadn't occurred to Charlie to call for a carriage. It hadn't occurred to him that they might need one. Working with Florin during the Jack case, she had been seemingly happy to walk everywhere with him. Now, after a pointed comment from Jasper on their way out, he wasn't sure if it was proper to make a lady walk. It was a fair consideration. He had tried getting around in ladies' dresses before, and it was always inhibiting and heavy. However, Florin seemed to move very well in her attire. She did everything well, and he had a horrible feeling that if he tried to raise the issue of the carriage with her, he would end up saying that in an inappropriate way.

They had been admitted when they had knocked but told there would be a wait. Given that they were showing up unannounced that seemed perfectly reasonable. They sat to wait in the parlour with tea and Charlie found the silence and social pleasantries even more uncomfortable than normal. It didn't make any sense. Previously, he had been unusually comfortable with Florin's company. That no longer seemed to be the case, and she certainly wasn't comfortable with him. He could tell.

She was notably flushed and troubled. She had been that way when she had arrived at the studio. At first, he had thought it relevant to whatever her reason for visiting, perhaps the news she brought. Then he had assumed her discomfort arose from the misunderstanding regarding his lie, until they set that straight. He did not expect her to be over it immediately, but he also didn't expect this reaction. She acted like it was nothing and brushed away all other attempts at apology, yet she was obviously distressed and trying hard to be patient with him. He recognised the behaviour.

The tension kept him from the tea. He would fidget with the cup, tap it inevitably. It was safer to stim the buttons on his coat and watch the world outside the sheer lace curtain. That should have helped more. It didn't. He was so painfully aware of her body in the chair next to his, like he could feel the heat coming off her.

"Penny for your thoughts, Florin?" he asked, trying to ease the atmosphere of the room.

"I'm thinking about… about Julian and his poetry," she replied.

A slight flounder. A half lie. She was so good at those. The first day they had spent chasing down the Jack's trail together and Florin had lied the whole way, mostly to herself. She couldn't help it. Just like he couldn't help noticing. He shouldn't pry though.

"I had no idea he was such a romantic," she commented.

"Hopelessly," Charlie admitted. "Julian had a rough time of it growing up. He came to London full of dreams — helpless, woeful dreams of love and desire and the storm of endless longing that transcends the boundaries of death."

She watched him for a moment, blinking slowly, and picked up her teacup. Her eyes were still tense with the heat in her cheeks, and he realised he had completely failed to ease the situation.

"I can see why you two are friends," she commented.

"He's fierce but he's kind," Charlie replied. "I like him, and I love the way he and Michael love each other. It's good for them. Skipp was always..." Charlie trailed off, searching for the right word. He realised the discomfort was easing. He was just talking, but whatever he was doing, it was working. "Skipp was always distant. I think that's just the way he is. I'm one of a few people he let get close, but I think that was mostly because he was curious to have found someone perceivably stranger than him. He needs someone like Julian, someone so wild and passionate and headstrong that he can't push them away, someone who will rip their hands bloody tearing down any walls Mike tries to build around himself and act like that's normal."

Amy laughed. It was a light, soft laugh, but Charlie looked to her in confusion. Laughing at that didn't make sense to him, not that he wanted to judge in any way. He just didn't know how to behave around her anymore, if he ever had. Looking back, perhaps his comfortable understanding of her presence had been a delusion. Perhaps they were very separate worlds colliding, and she had always just been laughing at him. At least her laughter always seemed affectionate, but maybe that was just the way she was.

Footsteps sounded in the doorway, and Lady Sterling strode into the parlour. She was far more composed than the last time Charlie had seen her, screaming bloody murder at her soon-to-not-be-daughter-in-law. Sterling's grey hair was pinned up in perfect fashion and she wore peacock blue like everyone should be so lucky to look upon the colour.

"Ah, my detectives!" she beamed at them. "Thank you for coming so quickly. I wasn't sure the two of you would be working this afternoon. When I spoke to you, Doctor, I wasn't sure when you'd have time to pass my message on, but I'm glad you speak so regularly. Very convenient for us clients."

"Lady Sterling," Amy rose politely. Sterling waved her back into the chair as she joined them at the table. Amy glanced at Charlie who had made no move to stand as the Lady entered. "Apologies for my associate—"

"Not at all, Doctor," Sterling smiled wryly. "By his standards, this is good manners. You should see him anytime I visit Susan. Poor girl spends half her time telling him to stop slouching."

"I'm not slouching!" Charlie protested.

"For once," Sterling eyeballed him.

Charlie tipped his head back and held in a groan. It was like having a crotchety distant aunt.

"Don't look so dour, Mister Shilling, I want to thank you," Sterling told him as she settled in the chair across from them. "I'm grateful for what you did for my family yesterday. You helped us all dodge a large bullet. I knew that bitch was trouble — pardon the language, Doctor."

"Believe me, Lady Sterling, I've said much worse about my last fiancé," Florin replied.

"Quite." Sterling gave her a sympathetic look. "Dare I take 'last' to mean there's a new someone on the horizon?"

Amy laughed. "No, my Lady. I've been betrothed my whole life and, given how that turned out, I rather think it's time I relished my freedom." She said it boldly, but there was a tight pain at the corners of her eyes. "If only it were so easy," she added, picking up her tea and sipping it.

"The heart wants what the heart wants," Sterling agreed sympathetically.

Charlie stared like he knew he was missing something. He certainly felt like he was, and his brain ran through the facts quickly. Florin still hurt over Harry. That made sense. She would probably feel that pain for many years to come, if not her whole life. Then, of course, there was Lizzie. Sterling's son was not the only one reeling from love lost yesterday. Charlie hadn't said anything to Florin about that. He worried if he said something she would think he was spying on her, but if he didn't say something was that insensitive? He didn't know what to do when friends were dealing with heartbreak. This was why he'd avoided her for two months, which was also a large part of why the situation was so bad now. He wanted to say something. The pain in her eyes made his stomach hurt, but that seemed like a bad statement to start with.

"Mister Shilling?" Sterling said pointedly.

"Yes?" Charlie tore his eyes from Amy's face to pretend he'd been listening the whole time.

"You saw the diamonds get taken?" she inquired.

"I saw a rather generic man — brunette, pale but ruddy complexion, high forehead, in a dark suit — leave the hall before the wedding," Charlie recounted. "He looked like he slipped something small from the gifts table. When I went to look I could see the trace of a small blue box that had been there and been removed recently, so I deduced the man had taken the box. What was in it, I cannot say, but it can't have been overly heavy. The indent on the tablecloth was light."

"I packed that box myself, Mister Shilling," Sterling told him. "It contains a velvet bag of diamonds that were to be a wedding gift for Annette — may the devil defecate upon her lying, cheating soul. They were a collection from different retired pieces throughout the family, and Annette and I had discussed my giving them to her to be fashioned into a new piece of her design once she was married into the family."

"Extremely generous of you, my Lady," Florin commented.

"And now they're gone," Charlie added.

"And now they're gone," Sterling repeated in that special shade of outrage only the aggrieved wealthy could truly capture.

"Only you and Lady Merrill knew about the diamonds?" Charlie asked. "No one else knew?"

"She may have told others, but I certainly didn't," Sterling defended. "I made sure they were wrapped discreetly and that no one would know what was in the box — save for Annette. They were disguised as a set of fine coasters. Besides, who on Earth would take from a gift table?"

Charlie chose not to answer that question. A better question would have been 'why did Sterling not just hand the gift over to her future daughter-in-law?' but he knew rich people did crazy things. Clearly, Sterling had believed her disguised gift safe from the rabble, given the 'quality' of guests invited to the wedding. Well, the standard they set for the most part anyway.

"I noticed a name was added to the guest list for the ceremony at the last minute," Charlie raised. "Phillipe Balles?"

"Yes, I recall," Sterling nodded. "Annette had him added last minute, but I never met the man. Second or third cousin I believe she said he was."

"I guarantee you, Sterling, they are not related," Charlie insisted.

"You think he's the man that took the diamonds?" she demanded.

"I've never met him, and I don't know what he looks like, but it's a good place to start," Charlie conceded. "Of recent years he's been working with a woman named Lucille Bonheur."

"Not a name I'm familiar with," Sterling confessed.

"She goes by many names," Charlie admitted. A hot and guilty flush erupted in his stomach, prickling through his body and up the back of his neck. He glanced weakly at Florin, but she showed no comprehension. Her ethereal green eyes watched him curiously over the rim of her mug in a way that made his stomach flip-flop and fan the uncomfortable fire in his chest. "Penny Farthing? Solange Franc? Caitlin Pence? Celia Dime?" He really didn't want to recite the next name on his internal list.

"Caitlin Pence…" Sterling mused. "That name I have heard. I think she was on Annette's list but something happened and she couldn't make it."

"So she sent Balles instead?" Amy deduced.

"Possibly." Charlie twisted his ring in thought. "But that still puts us at a setup, not a robbery. If Merrill invited Bonheur to the wedding but Bonheur couldn't make it, why would she then change the invite to Balles? Merrill must have known she was giving the diamonds to Bonheur and done whatever was necessary to make that happen."

"That thieving little —" Sterling began.

"But why?" Charlie sighed.

"Merrill's wealthy but she was marrying into money," Florin commented. "Provided she was faithful to her husband, she would have been a very rich woman, yet she was carrying on an affair. Let's save some time for now and assume she was paying off blackmail. Besides," she gave Charlie a look, "there's no way Merrill will speak to you after yesterday."

Charlie fidgeted with his ring and contemplated this. Florin wasn't wrong, Merrill wouldn't speak to him now. Blackmail was the most likely option, but not the only one. If he was going to get the diamonds back for

Sterling, he was going to need to trace the trail between Merrill, Balles, and Bonheur. Not impossible... but where to start?

"Who was in charge of the invites?" Charlie asked.

"I was," Sterling replied. "I was paying for most of it, so everything came through my people."

"Do you still have the address you sent Caitlin Pence's invite to?" he asked.

"I'm sure I can have someone find it for you," she answered. "If you think that's the best place to start."

"You want the diamonds returned and you said I could name my price?" Charlie recalled, settling back in the chair and running one fingertip repeatedly around the seal on his ring.

"Within reason, detective," Sterling warned.

"I want half the worth, plus expenses," he told her.

"Oh, do you now?" She raised an eyebrow.

"You need me for this more than I have any need to do it, and you can afford it," he said. "How much are the family's diamonds really worth to you?"

Sterling considered this, but she didn't consider it long. He knew she wouldn't. Half the worth was easily within her range. These were stones she'd been prepared to part with as a gift, after all. Now it was about the pride. Merrill had cheated her son and stolen from her, she wouldn't settle for anything less than getting even. The adultery was a war she could wage privately, but recovering her stolen property called for him, and they all knew it.

"You drive a steep bargain, Mister Shilling," Sterling sniffed. "Susan warned me about hiring you."

"And yet you're doing it anyway," Charlie smiled.

"She told me your prices can be outrageous, but that you have never not delivered," the old lady sighed. "I imagine Doctor Florin here knows all about that."

"Credit where credit's due," Charlie countered, not wanting to let Sterling put Florin on the spot. "I could not have caught the Jack without Florin, and I certainly wouldn't have survived the ordeal without her."

"Commendable," Sterling agreed. "And I suppose the rates are more reasonable for two."

Charlie did not consider them for two. He hadn't thought of that, but it was too late to try and raise the price now. That would look unprofessional. Besides, this was all to protect Florin's good name. She wasn't actually working the case with him.

"I shall have someone find you the address," Sterling announced, standing again and sweeping from the room. "Speed is of the essence, Mister Shilling! I needn't remind you that the further they get, the less likely it will be that you will find them all — and I am paying you to recover them all!"

The waited long enough to get the address, but Shilling was grateful to be out the door again when they were finally released. He stepped into the sunshine with Florin on his heels. Whatever had been going on when they arrived seemed to have settled, and the company was comfortable again. Charlie slid his thumb inside the folded scrap of paper and spread the note open. He grinned at it.

"Oh?" Florin queried his expression.

"Last known address is in Paris," he replied. "I was

confident she was in France, but France is a big place. Paris is nice and convenient, easy to get to."

"Paris is also big," Florin reminded him.

"Not as big as France, and I have an exact address," he grinned.

"How do you know this woman, Charlie?" she asked.

It was the worst question she could possibly have put to him. He could feel himself blushing as his brain scrambled for an answer. He couldn't tell the truth, not the whole truth, but they were still trying to recover from the last lie he'd told. He decided to stick to something that wasn't a lie.

"I keep an eye on a few select people around the globe who I have deduced to be perpetrators of a series of London cold cases," he admitted, unable to meet her eye and desperately stimming his coat buttons. "It was something I took up years ago for your father…"

"So you know she's a thief, you saw the connection, and you're tracking it down… while getting well paid for it," she added as they strolled back down the street together. "I thought you did a lot of your work without charge."

"I do. The money's a farce," Shilling snorted. "I don't charge for the work, I charge what people can afford. Our fair Lady has as much money as the Queen and she can afford to pay for this. Then I give the money back to the community — charities and the like. Skipp helps me with that side of things."

"That sounds more like you…" she smiled softly. "Charlie, did you mean what you said back there?"

"Yes," he replied. After a second of thought he realised he wasn't sure which specific moment she was referencing, but he had meant everything he said.

She was grinning at him like she knew he had no idea what he'd just agreed to. Of course she did. Her brain moved just as fast as his. It was an undiscovered natural wonder. He doubted anyone had realised just how brilliant she was yet.

"Especially the sarcastic eyerolls?" she teased.

"Especially," he grinned. "What are you asking, Florin?"

"You said you couldn't have caught the Jack without me?" she reminded.

He contemplated for a moment, tipping his head to the side as he tried to work out how best to phrase his thoughts on the matter. She smiled at the action with such glowing affection it made thinking difficult. He ran the tip of a finger round and round a button, trying to clear his head.

"You did in a single night what I couldn't do in months," he said finally.

"I had the benefit of sharing a roof with the killer," she countered. "If you'd been the one living with Harry, he never would have made it through the first murder. You would have known he was up to something."

"Don't sell yourself short, Florin," he replied. "You were brilliant, and impressively logical in the face of great personal loss and trauma."

"You mean that, don't you?"

"Of course," he insisted, baffled by her need to ask. "I hate to think where this insecurity has come from,

Florin. You have a refreshingly sharp mind. Despite my personal failings at keeping in touch during these trying months, I do enjoy your company and your intelligence — it helps keep me on my toes."

He was rather proud of his statement. Explaining himself to people was one of the hardest things to do, but he felt he had expressed his feelings appropriately. He had taken his sisters' advice about telling Florin the truth and it was working so far. Hopefully he was mending the gap that had grown between them. She certainly wasn't still carrying the discomfort they had arrived at Sterling's with anymore. She was looking at him the way she had when they'd been working to catch Harry. That look made him want to behave heroically and hide under a table in equal measure.

"Then I want to work this case with you," she blurted. "I want to go with you to France."

"You what?" Charlie panicked.

"I feel involved now, Charlie," she told him. "I know it's not the same as last time, but if you think I can be helpful, if you think I'm useful, then I want to help."

"What about your medical work?" he raised carefully.

"It's all contract work," she shrugged. "I haven't taken an ongoing position anywhere yet. There's nothing keeping me here right now."

"What about your father?" he tried.

"I'll ask him, but I can't imagine he'll have any objections," she replied.

Charlie fell silent. It was a trap. He'd walked into a trap. He wasn't entirely sure how he'd done it, but in attempting to forge ahead on the noble path of good he had stumbled into a trap and was now hanging by his ankles with a knife to his throat. He had no idea how to get out of it.

"Charlie…?" she spoke his name hesitantly.

"I'm thinking…" he muttered.

They turned up the next street and he kept his eyes on the path ahead of him. He couldn't meet her eye, and he had a feeling she was starting to notice. Her patience, which moments before had felt boundless and warm, was chilling noticeably in the hot sun.

"I won't take a cut of your charity money, and I can pay my own way!" she insisted. "I just want to help solve the case! Please, Charlie!"

"I don't care about the money," he dismissed.

"Then what? If you really don't want me to go—" she began with biting disappointment.

"I'm thinking!" he repeated urgently, before she laid an even bigger trap. That would have been a bigger trap. He knew how these things worked. Social interaction was a trap. Everything was a trap. He began again with a calming sigh, trying to find appropriately safe and truthful words. "I am going after dangerous people, Florin. I don't want to put you in harm's way, and I don't want you to get hurt."

"That's very sweet, Charlie, but I can take care of myself," she told him.

"Yes, that's what I always say," he replied drily.

"What's that supposed to mean?" she asked.

"Well, do you believe me when I say it?" he countered.

She laughed. He was being perfectly serious and she laughed. He'd never found anything as amusing as she seemed to find him. It was no source of comfort.

"*Touché*," she conceded. "However, you haven't managed to get yourself killed yet, so you must be at least partially capable. Although, I will take credit for saving you from Harry. If we hadn't intervened, he would have murdered you. All the more reason for me to come and help you. We can watch each other's backs."

Checkmate. The knife slit across. He was doomed. There was no way to tell her she couldn't go without starting a fight and making things even worse than he'd made them yesterday. Unless…

"Tell Henry," Charlie insisted. "Tell him that Sterling has hired me to track Lucille Bonheur to Paris to recover stolen goods and see what he says. If he has no objections to you undertaking such a mission, then neither do I."

He startled as Florin grabbed his arm enthusiastically, clasping his hand with her own and squeezing affectionately.

"Thank you, Charlie! You won't regret this, I promise. We'll recover the stolen pearls and be back in time for the trial!"

He groaned inwardly at the memory of the trial. He would just as soon not be back for it, but it was too important to miss. They were the key witnesses and the ones who had solved the case and caught the Jack. They had to be there to help present the evidence — or at least so that Harry's lawyer could cross examine them in excruciating detail.

She didn't let go of his hand as they walked, and he started to worry that his palm was sweaty. Her glove was soft against his skin and her fingers firm as they intwined with his. He had never held hands with anyone in public, not without dragging being involved. He worried that it was inappropriate, but he didn't want to let go either. She was standing so close he could smell her perfume, the same one from his pillow, and it was like a comfort blanket around his soul.

For a moment, he even entertained the idea of her walking the streets with him like this in Paris, but he quickly threw the notion from his mind like a lit firecracker. She couldn't come with him for this. It would be a disaster. At least there was no way Henry would let her go once he heard what the mission was.

7

"Of course you can go if that's what you think is best," Henry shrugged.

They were sitting together at the dinner table, trying desperately to ignore the empty seat that still felt strange after months of absence. Amy had explained that she and Charlie had been hired by Sterling to track down Lucille Bonheur and recover what had been stolen at the wedding. After a rough jibe that Lady Sterling's son's dignity was not going to be recovered in France, Amy had extrapolated for her cheeky father. He had agreed. She had left out how dangerous Charlie had said it would be, because that wasn't overly important.

"Why do I feel like I know that name...?" Henry mused, carefully dissecting his roast beef and potatoes. "Lucille Bonheur...?"

"Charlie said she was one of the cold case thieves he keeps an eye on for you," Amy said.

"Oh, Charlie said this, did he?" Henry teased softly, his massive grey eyebrows slanting at her.

"Daddy don't do that," she huffed.

"I'm surprised you two are talking again," Henry commented. "Yesterday you told me that he lied to you, after not speaking to you for two months."

"Yes…" she recalled. "I rather think that was… well… I guess a bit of a misunderstanding…"

"God Almighty, if that isn't a word I've heard in conjunction with his name as long as I've known the boy," Henry sighed. "He seems to crash from one misunderstanding to the next with absolutely everyone he meets."

Amy said nothing for a moment and ate quietly. That was probably a fair assessment, but she didn't like hearing it. Logic told her that the common factor proved Shilling was the problem, but he was sweet and well-intentioned, if a bit dopey, and she rather felt that everyone else misunderstanding him was the problem.

"Daddy…" she began softly. "Shilling is welcome in the house, isn't he…?"

"Why do you ask?" Henry raised an eyebrow.

"Just… just what he said today," she sighed. "He apologised for lying and avoiding us. He said he'd been staying away because he thought we wouldn't want to see him again after everything that happened — that he brought shame and bad luck to our door, ruined our lives, and we'd loathe him for it and want to pretend he didn't exist."

"He was not the one who brought scandal down upon us," Henry replied cuttingly, attacking his food. "He was not the one who ruined anything — except possibly your graduation party, but timing was never the boy's forte." Henry sliced his food like it had mortally offended him. His lips were pinched into a sneer and his nostrils flared.

Amy watched him painfully, unsure what to say. She felt a sudden understanding for why Charlie had kept his distance. She sometimes wished she could stay away too, but this was her life now, watching her father crack. And crack he did. His cutlery hit the plate with a light clatter. He covered his face with his hands and rested his elbows on the table. Amy could hear the deep and painful sigh behind his fingers.

"Daddy...?" she whispered, hesitantly reaching towards him, but staying her touch.

"You know, I miss him..." Henry murmured thickly, his voice surprisingly steady. "I miss him more than I thought I would. I miss the way things used to be."

Amy could feel tears in her eyes as her throat closed up. She wanted it to stop hurting, but it wouldn't. It had been months, and it just wouldn't stop hurting. Her father wouldn't talk about Harry, wouldn't even say his name, and the loss of it had been crushing them tighter every day.

Henry sighed deeply and rubbed his weary brow.

"I never thought I'd miss the scamp," he muttered. "Never thought... but I swear I had him dragged into my office — into the house even — once a month at least. Mad as a monkey on amphetamines, always spouting treasonous gibberish that we'd have to ignore for the greater good — because he always got the culprit. I know I'm hard on the boy, God herself knows someone ought to be, but he always got his man. I miss those days. I miss his ludicrous reports that would only make sense once he put all the pieces together. I miss the normality."

Amy stayed silent. That had taken a surprising turn. Or, perhaps, not so surprising. He still wouldn't talk about Harry. Still wouldn't acknowledge him. But, perhaps, his only way of talking about it was to reminisce on what else he had lost. Perhaps he would talk about Shilling because he couldn't talk about Harry. It made her uncomfortable, but she didn't know what to do or say.

"So, the two of you are gallivanting off to France on another crime-catching caper?" he looked to her, forcing a tone of joviality and pretending like he hadn't nearly broken apart at the dinner table.

"Yes Daddy," she replied softly. "But only if you don't need me here. I can stay if you need — Charlie is obviously more than capable—"

"Nonsense," Henry huffed. "*Charlie*," he leant on the name to tease her again, "wouldn't have asked you to go if he didn't need you. He's a stubborn wee goat like that. And it will be good for you to get out for a bit, get away from all this God-awful press and those obscene reporters."

She did not disagree. It certainly sounded refreshing.

"As long as you're all right," she insisted. "We won't be gone long. The trial starts next week, so we only have a handful of days at the most."

"Between the two of you, I'll be surprised if you haven't cracked the case in twenty-four hours," he chuckled. "I'm glad you've found something you want to do, darling. Possibly unexpected, but it's nice to see. It was starting to feel like you were only doing things because you felt you ought to."

"I admit my passion for medicine isn't what it once was," she conceded. "I hope it will come back, but the last couple of months…"

"I understand," he assured, possibly cutting her off before she could finish the sentence.

She didn't begrudge him that. Maybe she should have, but she understood his inability to discuss it, even if it wasn't doing them any favours. Besides, he was her dad. She couldn't treat him or advise him like he was a regular patient. He was still the boss and they still needed time.

"Amelia…" he said softly.

She looked to him and met his eye inquisitively.

"As long as you want to see him, Shilling is welcome here," he assured her.

"Thank you, Daddy," she smiled. "And I'm sure, if you want to see him, we can find some officers who would happily drag him kicking and screaming through the doorway."

He laughed and nodded appreciatively. Neither of them even had to imagine it, they'd seen it happen often enough. She could still remember a young Shilling being hauled in by the collar of his coat; dirty, scruffy, and completely unkept, screaming about class oppression and elitist kidnapping. At the time it hadn't been cute at all, but her current understanding of his person allowed her to look back on it fondly.

Speaking of looking back on things fondly, she remembered her trip to Charlie's studio that morning. Her face flushed as she recalled the look Julian had given her when he had caught her staring, like he wasn't probably guilty of doing the exact same thing once. In her mind, it was almost hard to reconcile the half-naked potter with the irate anarchist that used to get dragged into her father's office. Although, they did both have dirt in common. As well as messy straw hair, and serious grey eyes, and that sweet, crooked smile…

"Amy?" Henry asked.

"Thank you for understanding about France," she blurted. "You're right, it will do me some good to get away from the papers."

"Of course," he nodded supportively. "I promise not to have Tanner drowned while you're gone, but I swear some days it will be a close-run thing."

"Don't let him get to you," she advised. "He has more enemies than the Devil. You won't need to be the one who cracks first. I need to know you'll be okay if I'm gone for a week."

"I'll be fine, darling," he assured. "Just promise me you'll stay out of trouble."

"Mhm," she nodded obediently, a faint guilty flush lighting her stomach. She pushed it down. Between her and Charlie they had taken down the Jack of Hearts, London's most notorious and dangerous serial killer. By comparison, how dangerous could a couple of thieves be?

They caught the train to Dover the next morning and Charlie insisted on billing Sterling for both their tickets.

He still couldn't believe Henry had agreed to let Florin go with him. It was madness. He had nearly grabbed his Lordship by the lapels and shaken him over the tracks, except that he wasn't physically capable of lifting a man nearly twice his size in that manner and he would have had to explain the behaviour, which would have made it impossible to keep the truth from Florin.

So here he was, sitting on a train, hurtling towards disaster, and unable to think of any way out of it. Unless he could distract Florin with something when they got to Paris, he was going to have to introduce her to Lucille Bonheur. Maybe he could just play dumb? But then Bonheur would have to play dumb too, and that seemed rather unlikely.

He slouched in his chair, elbow against the window, chin in his hand, and tapped and fidgeted uncontrollably. The bruise across his knuckles ached. Somehow, the memory of getting it felt worse. He had tried to lament his situation to Julian and Michael the night before. Julian had taken it as well as he ever did, and Charlie had not been in the mood. They had been back in Mike's room, with their Skipper lounging at his desk perusing daily reports. Charlie had mentioned his concerns and made the mistake of repeating Florin's suggestion of watching each other's backs in Paris.

What had followed was a deliberately misheard jibe from Julian about washing, followed by his hysterical laughing while Charlie pinned him to the bed and beat him with an enthusiasm usually exhibited by law enforcement. He was pretty sure it was a strike to Julian's shoulder that had bruised his hand, but he hadn't noticed until much later. At the time, he had been far too incensed by Julian laughing like he was being tickled.

Michael, characteristically, hadn't looked up from his notes, and his efforts to placate them had consisted of the most sarcastic and monotonous tone imaginable protesting:

"No. Stop. Please. Won't someone think of the children."

Which had made Julian laugh harder.

When Terry had opened the door on them to demand what the racket was, he had taken one look at the room and decided it was actually best not to ask. Which, fortunately, had taken some of the flustered wind from Charlie's sails. Until, of course, Julian had reignited it.

"Really, Sleuth?" he had cackled, sitting up once Charlie climbed off him. "Driven to violence? What happened to two wrongs don't make a right?"

Charlie smacked him, open palm, on the nose. It had been enough to make the comedian wince and clutch his face. Which in turn had been enough to elicit a small chuckle and passing comment from Mike.

"She must have gotten right up your skirt, Charlie, to get you in such a fizz."

Julian had dissolved into further hysterics.

"You rogues leave me with no power but violence!" Charlie had huffed. "And I will keep hitting him, Skipp."

"Well, I'm not the detective, but I think he's enjoying it," Michael smirked. "Careful with your enthusiasm,

Swift. I might get jealous."

"Save your envy, Mikey. I'm not a fan of the punching," Julian admitted, rubbing his arm. "He's surprisingly strong, but the reaction is hilarious. I'll be the first to admit I deserve it, but, really Sleuth, it's not like you to be short on words."

"Bearing in mind that this is the woman he kissed before running into a doorway and having her fiancé arrested," Michael reminded.

"Harry was incarcerated as a serial killer and I don't know how you can make jokes about that," Charlie had countered.

"We're not," Michael replied. "We're just teasing you because you fancy her, Charles. I thought I had dangerous taste, but you, my friend, have really taken the cake."

"I don't fancy her, I respect her," Charlie glowered. "There is a steep difference."

"The doorway disagrees," Julian quipped. "It's in the same queue as your bright pink cheeks, tied tongue, and eager fists. You wouldn't care about Florin and Bonheur like you do if you weren't desperately invested in Florin's wellbeing. You care about her, Sleuth."

"Contrary to public opinion, I care about most people, and I don't like being teased!" Charlie protested, still deeply submerged in his denial. "That doesn't mean anything else. You're supposed to be my friends, and I have come to you with my troubles, and all you do is mock me about going to Paris with Florin. Besides, the kiss was part of the ruse to trap Harry. It was her idea, not mine."

"I don't think that's as true as you think it is, Sleuth…" Julian replied.

Julian and Michael had shared a look then. That look still haunted Charlie, who had tied a rock to his own ankles in the ocean of denial and refused to surface. He was the one who had been there. Florin had understood the need to provoke and fluster Harry into making a mistake. That's all any of that had been. She was a woman of rare intelligence and he respected that. Skipp and Swift seemed to think otherwise, and their shared glance had spoken an entire novel that Charlie steadfastly refused to read.

Except now his hand hurt and he was on a train of doom, heading South. The eyes of his friends were judging him across time and space, like they knew something he didn't. Consolation should have come from the knowledge that he was smarter than them and this was his life and his feelings, so of course he knew better. Somehow, that was exacerbating the anguish. An anguish already aggravated by Florin's stoic green gaze. He had seen those sharp eyes note his bruise and demeanour and whatever else she could decern that he wasn't even sure about.

Florin sat across from him, skirts arranged neatly over her crossed legs. She had a book open on her knee and her eyes cast down to it. Her curls were pinned up but spilled down the side of her neck. In the flickering sunlight, her auburn hair looked like autumn leaves against the smooth trunk of a dark oak. He didn't even realise he was staring until she looked up. Her eyes met his with a questioning glance. He looked away sharply.

His friends were still wrong. He hadn't really been staring, and if he had been, it was their fault.

"What's troubling you, Charlie?" she asked.

He shrugged and shook his head, willing the question away. He didn't have the spare energy to think up an answer. She wasn't going to accept it. He could tell from her eyes that not answering wasn't an acceptable reply. She had that set to her shoulders, in the way she held her head; he was about to get lectured. That was a familiar look. Everyone important in his life gave him that look eventually. It was nice to think she was important now too, but in a respectful and collegial way. Florin folded her book closed on her lap. Charlie scanned the title upside down.

"Good book," he commented, before she could scold him. "One of their best," he alluded to *Dawson & Kropp*.

Florin gave a soft smile and a nod.

"Yes," she agreed. "I discovered all my favourites are Alice Jones stories."

Shilling cocked his head to the side and regarded her curiously, impressed. Her smile widened, but she turned her face down, as though embarrassed by his admiration. Her demure blush didn't change the way he looked at her. As far as he was concerned, she had no need for that kind of modesty. Also, she was right, the Alice Jones stories were the best. That wasn't even opinion anymore. He was thoroughly convinced it was fact. Florin had good taste. In everything, really.

"I hunted them down," she admitted bashfully. "All the ghost writers. I... I think I just wanted to see if I could, after you said you'd done it. Besides, it wasn't like I had a lot else to do these past couple of months. It wasn't hard to skim through my collection, divide up the books, and then trace information back through the publishers."

"And it took you less than two months," he grinned.

"I had a head start," she shrugged. "You told me how many I was looking for."

"Very clever, Florin," he praised, delighted he knew someone else mad enough and brilliant enough to engage in his hobbies. A very faint niggle in the back of his mind sounded like Julian laughing at him, but he wrestled it into silence. He would not be undone here, not by the gossip and speculation of busybodies who had nothing more worthy with which to occupy their time.

"I've actually been writing my own..." she admitted, a soft blush tinging her expression. "I'm not sure how it holds up to the other writers, or what I'll do with it when it's finished. I suppose I'm mostly just writing it for me..."

Charlie wasn't sure why hearing that felt like being choked, but his oesophagus was definitely closing up. Maybe it was an allergic reaction. He cleared his throat carefully and tried to behave like everything was normal.

"I'd love to read it, if you want any other eyes on it," he offered.

"I think I'd like that..." She nodded slowly. "Lizzie told me I should show it to you." Florin blushed harder. "I... uh, I've been visiting her..."

"I know," he told her, trying to put her out of her

discomfort. "Julian told me."

"It's over now," she blurted. "We're not seeing each other anymore."

"I know," he admitted. "Julian told me."

Florin gave him a look. Charlie grimaced. He felt like he shouldn't have said it, but he wasn't going to lie to her about it. Her expression settled ever so discreetly from indignation to tolerance. He watched the subtle change with an attentiveness that would have sparked a comment from Skipp and Swift, and made a mental note never to tell them.

"What a gossipy little bitch," she cursed under her breath.

Charlie laughed. He tried to stifle it, but at the cost of bringing tears to his eyes. Florin smiled at him as he struggled to breathe.

"I'm sorry, I know he's your friend," she commented.

He waved her off, still struggling to speak at the matter-of-fact way she had hit the nail so cleanly on the head.

"He is a gossipy little bitch," Charlie gasped. "You have no idea."

"Well, I have some idea now," she replied haughtily. "How it's either of your business, I've no idea."

Charlie blushed. There was nothing to be done about it. She was right and he felt like a snoop.

"It's not," he admitted apologetically. "I guess... well... obviously Julian is a gossip, and... and I suppose he knows I have been concerned about you." Now why did he go and say that?

"You've been concerned?" she smiled.

"Well… uh, after… after everything…" Charlie stammered.

"I'm all right, Charlie," she assured him. "But thank you for caring."

"Of course, Florin. Always," he nodded.

The answer seemed to placate her in an unusually contented way. Her eyes lowered to the book cover for a moment as the slightest shy smile touched her lips. It was the look of a second and it wasn't one he knew how to translate. She glanced back to him coyly.

"So, are you going to tell me what you did to your hand?" she asked, no longer beating around the bush.

"Oh. Julian," he answered. "Gossipy little bitch."

"What did he say?!" Florin exclaimed.

Charlie considered not answering, but that really didn't feel like it would help the situation.

"He made an unseemly remark about us travelling to Paris," he replied.

"And you hit him?!" she cried. "Charlie, that's so unlike you."

"He was the first to admit he deserved it," Charlie defended. "But he's bony, so it hurt."

"You didn't fall out over it, did you?" She hesitated in concern.

"God, no," Charlie sighed. "He laughed the entire time I hit him and I have every confidence he was going to coax Skipp into kissing it better once I was gone. I'm just grateful he was prepared to let me leave before they got started. Julian can be quite the exhibitionist."

"Somehow that doesn't surprise me," Florin

commented. "I'm still surprised you hit him though. I thought you had a policy to never be the one to start a fight."

"It wasn't a fight, it was an ineffective beating," Charlie replied. "And I didn't start it, he did. It was an unseemly comment, Florin. Unseemly."

"Can I know what he said?" she asked.

"No." He went scarlet with the memory and the notion.

She laughed at him, a subtle and knowing twinkle in her eye, and turned back to her book, flicking the pages open. He watched her read for a moment, before realising he was watching and quickly turning away. He couldn't even observe her without blushing. Obviously, this would wear off with time. It just felt like Julian's mockery was running through his mind dropping lit matches. The jibe was still fresh and hot. It sparked the imagination. A sudden picture of Florin in the bath startled him to look back at her, reality quashing the fantasy. He didn't *want* to be thinking of Florin this way. Other people had put the idea in his head and it was uncomfortable. Unfortunately, now that he had thought it, it was also unforgettable.

8

There was rain over the Channel when they got on the ferry. Amy felt confident that Charlie had been hoping for brisk sea air and a view of the ocean, but he was cooped up inside with her and the other passengers. Travel seemed to make him even more skittish than normal. He hadn't stopped fidgeting all day. He twitched and blushed and flinched from her constantly. It almost certainly had something to do with what Julian had said, and she wanted to say something to put him at ease, but she had no idea where to start.

Besides, she couldn't help but wonder if she'd even disagree. Charlie was so easy to tease, and it was possible she would have laughed at Julian's comment herself. Given that it was likely a cheeky remark about the two of them being alone in Paris. She wasn't going to pretend to herself that she'd stopped thinking about him half-dressed in the morning sunlight at the pottery wheel, but it was Charlie. He'd probably never thought of anyone the way she knew she was starting to think of him. It wasn't fair to expect him to, and she tried to sympathise.

Sympathy felt empty when she could barely stop herself clutching at him. She wanted to take his hand to sooth his nerves, and straighten his hair, and smooth his coat. She wanted to link her fingers through his fingers and rest her head on his head and just make him relax for a moment, but she knew that none of those actions would help him at all. Undoubtedly the reverse.

So she kept a polite distance and gave him space. She let him fidget and twitch. But she watched and she smiled at the quirks. That seemed to make his anxiety worse, but she wasn't just going to ignore him.

As soon as the weather broke, he was out at the railing like a shot. She didn't take it personally, but she couldn't stop being curious. Her attempts to settle him with conversation and interrogate his issues on the train had been short lived, and perhaps it was time for another attempt.

She stalked out the door to the slippery walkway and approached him carefully. He was leaning on the railing, staring down at the waves as the boat cut through them. In the company she was used to, a gentleman would have given her a polite nod or tipped his hat. Charlie didn't even look up, but she knew he knew she was there. Appropriate social etiquette was not something she had ever expected of Shilling, even when she had only known him by reputation. He railed against society, protesting an endless barrage of perceived injustices. But watching him work, beginning that work herself, and watching her life fall apart, was starting to shine a light for her on all the ways he wasn't wrong.

"Florin," he muttered politely as she stopped at his side. He was hunched over the railing, leaning on his elbows, and twisting his father's ring like he was trying to unscrew his finger. It was a heavy, solid piece on his skinny, pale hand. The engraved cross gleamed when it caught the light every time it twisted back around.

"What's troubling you, Charlie?" she asked. "Really."

He was silent for a moment. They listened to the engine of the ship and the slosh of the waves. A gull cried somewhere in the distance. She knew better than to think he was ignoring her. Charlie just tended to take longer than others to process things, probably because he processed more. Amy liked to think part of it was because what he had to say carried deeper thought and weight.

"Do... do you ever think about your parents...?" he asked hesitantly. The ring went round again.

"Arguably, I still live with my father," she countered. "It's impossible not to think of someone when you see them every day."

Shilling didn't respond. That wasn't what he'd meant and they both knew it. He was going to wait until she answered the question he had actually asked. She sighed reluctantly.

"All right, Henry was only ever supposed to be my father-in-law," she admitted. "He was the father of my betrothed. Still, he's the man who raised me, along with a string of nannies. He's the only parental figure I've ever known. I never met Margaret. She died in childbirth..." Amy paused for a sick moment, letting the dread and despair pass through her and out the other side. "Maybe that's why Harry ended up the way he did…"

"No," Shilling countered with an uncharacteristic coldness.

She turned to look at him, at his serious profile glaring at the waves.

"My mother died in childbirth too. Harry and I have that in common. We never knew our mothers, but only one of us ended up a psychopath. Unless your professional medical opinion thinks that's the root of all that's wrong with me, he does not get to use that excuse," he insisted.

"There's nothing wrong with you, Charlie," she told him.

"Rebecca's going to get you to sign that in writing when we get back," he smiled ruefully. "She never passes up a chance to get doctors to declare me sane."

"You're eccentric, not insane," she smiled back. "Unlike my actual father…"

"He's not your father," Charlie scoffed. "Don't play dumb, Florin. You can't maintain it."

"Well, I don't know my birth parents, Shilling," she huffed. "My birth certificate lists Elizabeth Florin as my mother — which we both know is a fake name given by a woman who ran out on me — and David Pound as my father — which we both know was crossed out again as soon as they realised I didn't look like a Pound."

"Thank goodness," Charlie quipped. "God did you a favour there."

"Are you flattering me, Charlie?" she teased, a small aching part of her longing to have him say she was pretty.

He seemed to realise, and his cheeks flushed rose pink.

"Beauty is arbitrary," he commented. "Although, general consensus does not favour it in the Pound line and would concede that you have an unusual combination of attributes that extend a certain allure."

She decided to overlook 'unusual' in favour of 'allure' and gave up fishing. Charlie was not the sort of person one went to searching for compliments. Unless it was regarding intellect, and that was still as rare as a blue pig — which was probably why he made her feel special, and why she was still chasing more of the sentiment.

"You say that, but *general consensus* holds that Harry Pound is very attractive," she countered.

"Physically, maybe," Charlie shrugged. "I think he got his looks from his mother. The Pounds are notoriously wealthy, not handsome, and Harry is undoubtedly a Pound. A truly macabre victim of the Pound Madness."

"The Pound Madness?" she echoed.

"Runs in the family, if you trace it back," he assured. "Not homicidal behaviour, but insanity, certainly. Take Henry's younger brother, for example. I guarantee you, Florin, David Pound was mad as a cut snake before your mother got her claws in him."

"I suppose that's kind of you to say, but the pattern of damage appears to be hers," Amy sighed. "She married David and convinced him that I was his, right up until I was born, at which point she vanished in the wind along with most of his wealth. Being abandoned, betrayed, robbed… apparently, he lost the plot completely. Daddy had him committed and I was never allowed to go with him to visit. It does look like 'Liz Florin' did the damage."

"I won't pretend she helped his health," Charlie agreed. "But he was a fragile man with many flaws. Still is, I suppose. I'm not trying to make excuses for anyone, Florin. I was just curious. Apologies."

"You don't have to apologise, Charlie," she told him. Her eyes watched the waves as she contemplated his curiosity. Charlie was curious about everything. It wasn't unusual, and he had his reasons to dwell.

Henry was a cornerstone of her whole life. She couldn't imagine a world without him, and she pitied the man at her side for his loss, not that she'd ever tell him that. For people who didn't know him, she knew he came across as distracted and uncaring, but for the few who did, they knew he was so empathetic it hurt him. The fact that he'd kept his father's ring just proved his sentimentality.

"He misses you, you know," she sighed.

Charlie cocked his head to look at her. She almost laughed. God, she loved that look. That quizzical puppy face. It was one of the first mannerisms that had endeared him to her.

"Daddy," she elaborated. "He misses you. He misses having you dragged into his office to explain your mischief. Misses the way things used to be. I know why you've kept your distance, and I respect it, but I assure you it is wholly unnecessary. We don't blame you, Charlie, either of us, and you are still welcome under our roof."

He was quiet again for a moment, and she watched his serious face and lopsided frown fondly until he turned away, unable to hold her gaze.

"Perhaps more so than when Harry lived there…" he murmured, almost to himself, before perking up and turning back to her. "I'm not surprised to hear he misses how things used to be, but I am surprised he thinks I am what he's missing."

"Then be surprised, Shilling," she invited. "Be surprised that Daddy misses you. Be surprised that I am fond of you. Be surprised that I don't think or care about my birth parents —whomever they may be. Be surprised that you're welcome in our house, and that, despite your best attempts, you are far more agreeable a personality than you seemingly strive to be."

"I shall have to try harder," he mused at the clouds.

She elbowed him in the side. He laughed. The sound broke over the side of the boat, impish and shy. The cheeky uncertainty in it made her giggle. It struck her that they had never really laughed together before this trip. Life had always been much too bleak and serious. Perhaps that was why she was escaping it, chasing him to Paris. Both of them chuckled at his poor attempt at humour. He squinted up at the sky as thin drops of rain began to patter down around them.

"Come on, Florin." He put his arm about her shoulders. "Best not stand about in it."

A warm and pleasant flush spread through her chest at the touch of his arm around her, and she kept smiling to herself as she let him guide her inside, leaning into the comfort of his shoulder.

Night was falling when the train came into Paris. Shilling and Florin gathered their bags and caught a carriage to a hotel he knew by name, called The Blue Rose. He was insistent that they did not pursue the case until morning. Florin kept giving him strange looks he couldn't decipher, but she kept close and that was comforting. He noted as they travelled together that she hadn't changed her perfume. It had occurred to him that she might, after everything that happened with Harry leaving it on the bodies of his victims, but she still had that soothing scent that seemed to settle his unease.

He booked them separate rooms on the same floor of the hotel, all courtesy of Lady Sterling's wallet. The Blue Rose was a neoclassical building, well-kept and maintained to a standard he was comfortable housing Florin in. He might have found himself sleeping in hostels, abandoned dens, and jail cells through the years, but Florin had standards and Sterling's money could be well-spent meeting them. Besides, Charlie wasn't opposed to a good night's rest. He was just easily distracted from it.

She wouldn't let him take his bag upstairs and insisted on paying the groom to do it. His protests were silenced with a look. He was all for the working class getting paid, he was all for doing the paying, but the bag wasn't heavy and he was perfectly capable of carrying it. Mostly, he wasn't for the class system, and refused to be waited on, unless Florin glared at him hard enough. Those sharp green eyes told him in no uncertain terms that there were places to fight his battles and this was not one of them. He didn't want to embarrass her, and knew enough to hold his tongue.

They took the elevator to the fourth floor. It would have been easy enough to walk, but Charlie wanted to drive home his point about how easy it would have been to take the bags, and the rattling clank of the metal cage covered their conversation as she asked about the case.

"The address Sterling gave us isn't far from here," he told her. "Only a few streets over."

"Do you have a map?" she asked.

He tapped his temple, checking the address again and cross referencing it with his own notebook for the case. Florin was giving him a look.

"How well do you know Paris?" she asked him.

"I've only visited twice," he admitted, flicking back a page in his notes. "But I memorised the map."

"You memorised the map?" she echoed.

He nodded.

"Of the whole city?" she checked.

He nodded again.

"Charlie!" she exclaimed.

He startled at the sound of her voice and pocketed the notes, looking up in confusion. He wasn't sure why she was yelling at him, but her tone was exasperated. Hints of doubt. She always used his first name. It was very informal. She thought of him informally. He thought of her estimably. He looked over to her and cocked his head in inquiry. She started to laugh helplessly.

"Charlie, you can't have memorised an entire map of Paris!" she insisted. "That's impossible."

The elevator clanked into place and stopped. They stood for a second in the echo, and then Charlie unlocked the doors and pulled them open.

"Well, I did," he stated, clicking the cage doors back and motioning for Florin to leave first. "I had to, so I did. I'm very good with maps."

Florin didn't argue the point again. She stepped out and he followed, closing up the elevator loudly behind them. She didn't start up the corridor without him. When he turned, she was still waiting and watching. There was a set to her eyes that told him he was treading thin ice, but he had no idea what he'd done. This time it couldn't be his fault.

"So," she began as they set off slowly down the passage. "What do you know about the area Bonheur was staying?"

"Not her usual quality of abode," Charlie replied. "Probably just a place to lie low between cons. It's the sort of place she might have met Balles initially."

"A halfway house or a drug den?" Florin asked.

"Something like that," Charlie shrugged. "Part brothel too, I imagine. It was an aspiring High House at one point. Fell into disrepute. Don't know the exact state of it, but I'll find out more soon enough."

"Oh, will you just?" she queried.

"Yes..." He felt like it was a trap but couldn't see

where the danger hid. "That's what we came to Paris for."

"The trail that's growing colder every minute?" she reminded.

"Don't let it cause you stress, Florin," he smiled. "I'll get you settled and be right on it."

His back collided with the wall hard enough to bang, and he knocked the back of his head. She had him by the lapels and he was reminded of the alleyway back home when he had commented on the state of her engagement and sex life. She had that same daggered look in her eye as she pinned him down.

"Charlie, are you about to leave me in the hotel while you go and pursue the case alone?" she demanded like she already knew the answer.

"… No," he lied, very badly.

He actually heard the metaphoric ice crack and shatter beneath him. Huh, it was still his fault.

Her hands tightened on the front of his jacket. He could feel the pull and worried she would lift him, or worse — throw him. She could probably do it too. Not far, mind you, but he was not a big person and she was a strong woman.

A door near them opened and someone stuck their head out, startling at the sight of them. Florin stared them down and told them bitingly in French that this wasn't their business. Their startled eyes took the warning and they shut the door again tentatively. Despite being the man she had pinned to the wall, Shilling was impressed. She was so ruthless when she wanted to be. Her eyes found him again and, regardless of her stunning anger, he couldn't bring himself to cower.

"You're not getting rid of me that easily, Shilling," she warned him cuttingly. "If you didn't want me here, you should have said before we left."

"That would have upset you more," he replied, hanging limply in her grasp. "I don't want to hurt you, Florin. I don't want anyone else to hurt you either."

Her grip slackened. He didn't try and get free from it, but he slumped back against the wall and let his heart hammer gently beneath her hands. Her fingers tangled in his coat were warm against his chest and he could feel them suddenly weaken.

"There's a method to my madness," he tried to explain, when she didn't say anything. "I work the way I work, and I get results following my brain, but it isn't always safe. It's almost never safe. That's my choice and I'm loath to drag anyone else into it. I work alone. That's better for everyone. Safer for everyone…"

"Last time you ditched me to go after a suspect you nearly got yourself killed!" she reminded.

"Exactly!" he exclaimed. "Foolish behaviour, I'll concede, but if I had to do things again, Florin, I would do them the same way—" She clamped a hand over his mouth to silence him.

"Charlie, if you are trying to argue why you should be allowed to go gallivanting off alone, you are doing a tremendously awful job of it," she warned. "I'm touched that you're concerned for my wellbeing, but I think we both know the one of us who needs looking after is you."

He tried to argue, but she was still holding his mouth, so he stuck his tongue out and licked her palm. She recoiled with a yelp, letting him go and staring between her wet hand and his innocent expression, trying to reconcile that he had actually done something so disgusting and childish. If she really knew him at all, she would have known it was perfectly in character.

"I do just fine on my own," he huffed, straightening his coat and beating out the creases. "I've always done fine on my own. Florin, if anything happened to you, I'd never forgive myself, and your loved ones wouldn't forgive me either."

"How do you think I feel?" she replied.

"Irate that I'm trying to cut you out of a case for your own safety," he answered, mildly confused at so obvious a question. He tilted his head as he regarded her, an unconscious gesture of habit, but one he was starting to realise elicited some kind of reaction from her. She smiled at him.

"How do you think I'd feel if something happened to you, Charlie, and I wasn't there?" she clarified. "What do you think it would have been like for me if I had been a minute too late to Harry's office all those weeks ago and found him standing over your body?"

"I imagine that would have been a grim affair," he conceded.

"I'm here to make sure you don't get yourself killed chasing a fraction of a rich woman's wealth," she told him. "A task remarkably unaligned with your interests, so don't think I don't know something is afoot. We're solving this together, and we're looking out for each other, both of us. You don't get to cut me out, no matter how dangerous you think this is or whatever else you're hiding. I helped you take down Harry, I can take whatever this disaster is, and I'm not going to risk losing you over an old woman's treasure."

"You're in no danger of losing me, Florin," Charlie promised, wondering why on Earth he'd say something so stupid yet unable to stop himself from doing it.

"If you feel so confident you should have no issues with me accompanying you," she insisted.

"There are different kinds of danger…" he began tentatively, wondering if he was walking himself into a new hole.

"And you've heard where a woman scorned is ranked?" she tested.

He nodded. Somewhere out in the world, he knew Rebecca was suddenly and deeply proud of his ability to take a hint, especially one he'd nearly been beaten with. Florin accepted his nod, but she was barely placated. He caught the weary eye roll as she turned away. One cautious hand reached out to her, almost too late, but he caught her hand in his. She turned back in surprise. That surprise deepened as he took both her hands in his. He tried to meet her eye with sombre sincerity.

"Florin," he sighed. "I concede the battle, but please, whatever happens from here, don't say I didn't warn you."

Now it was her turn to be speechless. She wore it well, lips almost parted like she was convinced she had something else to say, and eyes wide with astonishment in a field of midnight black freckles. He didn't expect her to be so taken aback, but took the stunned awe on her face to mean that she understood the severity of what he was trying to say. At least he had gotten something right.

He let her go and moved to the door that matched the number he'd been given, fumbling in his pocket for the key. She was still watching him, but that was her prerogative. It wasn't like he was going to try running out on her, after all.

9

The night was dark and still. An ominous chill hung in the air. Every noise carried, amplifying the atmosphere. Amy kept her hand tucked in Charlie's elbow as they walked down the narrow, cobbled street. Their footsteps echoed off the looming buildings, and she couldn't help but notice hers were louder. Charlie walked softly, and he seemed unfazed by the lateness of the hour and the condition of the neighbourhood. She couldn't say anything though, not after her insistence that she be allowed to accompany him.

He barely seemed to be looking around, but she watched his eyes roam and knew he was seeing more than most. The notion that he could have memorised a map of Paris had been utterly preposterous, until she had remembered who he was, and what he did. Then she had gone out into the streets with him. He moved about the area like he was a native to it. It was Charlie Shilling, of course he'd casually memorised the streets of Paris. She watched him slow and stop, eyeing a building, and marvelled that his variety of insanity was a beautiful one.

The building in question was less than welcoming, despite the lamps hanging in the doorway and the light spilling down to them from the windows. At least the sporadic shrieks that leapt from the open windows spoke to pleasure over violence. Amy had no desire to enter, but she couldn't back out now. Besides, Charlie had that adorable, curious head tilt going and a look on his face that suggested this wasn't as bad as he had feared, even if it was the kind of disreputable dive that Amy would never have found herself near in ordinary circumstances.

It was also possible the clenching in her chest and racing of her heart had nothing to do with the possible danger they were walking into, and everything to do with how close he kept her. She wasn't sure she had recovered from their interaction in the hotel hallway. For all that he was observant, he had no idea what he did to her.

She kept a tight hold on his arm as they stepped through the front door. Light and laughter and an array of interesting scents spilled over them as they entered. Amy was suddenly and sharply reminded of the first time she had gone to a High House. This was very different, but the discomfort was the same. She was used to nudity in a medical sense. Sexual nudity was something she had been sheltered from, and she had worked hard to overcome her embarrassment since. Now, for some reason, it came roaring back.

Bronny's house was kept clean, hygienic, and stylishly modern. It had an air of cabaret about it. This place was none of that. The main hall was wide enough to be occupied and it was lit only by the leaking light of open doorways. Scatterings of scantily clad or naked occupants were strewn throughout the building, every single one reeking of the abuse of at least one substance. Part of her wanted to roll up her sleeves and start treating people. The other part knew these people did not want her help.

Raucous laughter burst from the first room they went by and she jumped, clutching Charlie's arm tighter and wishing she hadn't reacted. He hadn't. He was completely unfazed. She didn't know how he did it.

A woman loitered in the hallway, wearing nothing but an open robe slung about her shoulders. She saw them come in and leant teasingly against the wall, eyeing them sensuously as she asked them in French if the cute couple were looking for something special. Amy bit down mortified embarrassment but her face still flushed in the dim hall.

"Sort of," Charlie replied, utterly nonplussed and in English. "We're looking for a particular someone."

The woman stood straight and slung her robe on properly, eyeing them both up. Amy could see her trying to place them. There had been an instant wariness, but the English had thrown her.

"Police?" she checked, just in case.

Charlie shook his head. "No, Ma'am. We're here looking for Lucille Bonheur, although she goes by other nam—"

"Who asking?" she inquired.

Charlie paused. Amy wondered what he was going to say. They both knew he could be truly awful at lying, but the truth might not be wholly wise here either. Still, she was surprised how he could morph into someone different when he was working. He didn't balk or stutter, and the flicker of hesitation seemed so natural.

"Her daughter is trying to track her down," he answered.

The woman shook her head at them. She reached into her pocket and pulled out a cigarette, bumming a light from someone slightly further down the hall before turning back.

"Tell her not to bother," the lady warned.

"We would, but that's not what we were hired for," Charlie replied, waving away the smoke she blew at him. "We get paid to find Bonheur. If she isn't interested, that's someone else's problem."

"She not here anymore," the woman shrugged. "Been gone a while."

"What about Philippe Balles?" Charlie asked.

The woman gave them a shrewd look. She hadn't expected them to know about Balles. Charlie took a couple of coins from his pocket and subtly passed them to her. They disappeared into her robe and she nodded, taking an anxious drag on her cigarette. She jerked her head to indicate they should follow, and she set off deeper into the building.

They followed her to a room on the third floor. It was set back into the building with a small window that looked directly onto the neighbouring stone wall. The space was cramped and decaying. All the paint had begun to peel from the walls. The door was barely attached and couldn't close properly into its frame anymore. Everything inside smelt of must and mould.

The small fireplace was choked and overflowing with ash. Amy was immediately reminded of a prison cell.

"He stay here last," their guide told him, indicating into the room. "Those things are his. Haven't seen him since yesterday."

"*Merci beaucoup*," Charlie gave her a nod.

She returned the gesture and left them to it. If they were going to snoop, she was going to pretend she didn't know them or how they had found Balles' things. As soon as she was gone, Charlie detached himself from Amy's grip and fell upon the nest of blankets and possessions bundled in the corner. Personally, Amy would have beat it with a stick to check for rats first, but he didn't seem to find any.

"What are we looking for?" she asked.

"Anything," Charlie replied unhelpfully. "Anything that helps explain where or why he's gone — or why he bothered to come back here after returning from England."

Amy pursed her lips in thought and cast her eyes over the filthy room. She began to — how did Lizzie put it? — do a Charlie. He was right. They were looking for Balles because they knew he was the thief, even if he wasn't the mastermind. Asking for Bonheur first with a fake story helped throw off the scent. But if Balles had returned to Paris with enough diamonds in his pocket to buy a castle… what on earth was he doing coming back here? Yet, the lady they'd met downstairs said she'd seen him yesterday. That meant he had been here.

It certainly gave Amy cause to wonder. Why would someone with a new fortune return to the squalor they'd come from? He could have gone anywhere. He could have run off to a beach in the Mediterranean or vanished into the mountains in Germany. Why come back? You only came back if there was something you couldn't leave.

Charlie made a musing sound behind her.

"You found something?" Amy inquired, still slowly perusing the room.

"A ripped note," he answered. "Looks like part of an address."

Amy crouched by the fireplace, carefully stoking through the overflowing remains with the nearby poker.

"I might have found the rest..." she mused, collecting a few rough scraps that hadn't burnt. Given the condition of the fireplace she wasn't surprised parts had survived. Any fire someone tried to start in that mess without cleaning it would inevitably choke itself out.

She felt Charlie come over and squat down beside her as she dusted ash from the charred parchment. Unfortunately, three of the pieces were blank edges with no writing. Nonetheless, another one had 'to the church' scrawled on it in neat handwriting and another still 'return ticket to London. Anne—' in the same cursive. Charlie held out his piece against hers. Different paper and handwriting. However disappointing, it was almost to be expected.

"Well, he definitely received a letter about Merrill's wedding," Amy deduced from her scraps.

Charlie had a scrutinising look on his face. His soft

grey eyes were narrowed in thought and his crooked nose was contemplatively scrunched. Amy watched his face near her shoulder in the half light, wishing she could look away, yet seemingly unable to. Without saying anything, Charlie reached out slowly and plucked one of the scraps from her fingers. He held it near his note, but positioned both outstretched like he was holding a snake instead of paper. It made it easy for her to compare the two, although she wasn't sure what she should be inspecting beyond their clear differences. Charlie was glaring at them like the note had dared to keep secrets from him. She wondered for a moment if it was that simple, if he solved cases just by glaring at the clues until they caved to his adorably serious expressions. The thought made her want to laugh and she tried to push it down. It was silly of her to wallow in such distractions when she could practically hear his brain ticking at speed.

"I think I know where to go…" Charlie mused.

He'd solved it with two scraps of paper, and what she had to conclude was an utterly singular mind. Although, she still felt a strong urge to berate herself further.

The night was particularly dark in this part of town, and Shilling was surprised to find how grateful he was for the company. Florin was awfully good company, and she had saved him excellent time digging through the fireplace. The scrap of address he had found in one of Balles' pockets conjured to mind three possible locations in town, depending on the missing information that had been carelessly torn off. One was a private residence. One was a butcher's shop. And one was an abandoned church.

Shilling had taken an educated guess.

Now he was standing with Florin outside the overgrown gates looking at the crumbling old building and pondering if it was such a fantastic idea to drag a good woman into an abandoned church at midnight. Especially when the overgrowth on the gates had so obviously been recently cut through, and the gates so obviously hauled open, and the path to the broken main door so obviously trodden — by horses, nonetheless.

At least it meant they were in the right place.

His heart sank as Florin took a small lantern from her bag and lit it. There wasn't any going back now. Trying to dissuade her would just provoke her wrath.

"Stay close, Florin," he advised.

"Worry about yourself, Charlie," she replied kindly. "I'm not the one trouble keeps finding."

He cocked his head and narrowed his eyes. That was not true, although he took her point.

"I sincerely disagree..." he commented, following her carefully through the gate.

She gave a quiet, fond chuckle at his expression, and her eyes sparkled with humour in the light of the lantern as she glanced back. Not that he was looking.

"These vines look like they were cut only yesterday," she commented.

"It looks that way," he agreed.

"If we missed the meeting and Balles sold the diamonds, this trip might become a much bigger adventure," Florin whispered, following the tracks to the main door. "How do we reconcile that with the trial?"

"We cross that bridge when we get to it," Charlie replied carefully, hedging his own private suspicions. "Here," he offered, taking the lantern and holding her hand as she hitched her skirts to climb over the broken remains of the chapel door. He helped her across and followed her through, noting the breakage in the old wood. It had become soft and water damaged in its abandonment, but it had also been kicked in hard enough to splinter it about the same time the vines on the gate had been cut. Most people did not kick in doors for the fun of it.

Inside the church, the scent of mould and decay was strong. Florin pulled a handkerchief over her face. Shilling didn't blame her. He cast the lantern over the broken down remains of the building, sending a family of rats scurrying from the light. Half the roof was gone, and what was left had bats nesting in it. Animal filth covered the floor and the broken, rotting pews.

"Who would agree to meet in a place like this?" Florin mused, aghast. She took the lantern back and held it high, casting the light over the ruins of the well-looted building.

"People who don't want anyone accidentally stumbling onto their affairs..." Shilling replied, stepping carefully through the muck and watching the dark corners of the floor.

"Something happened here," she pointed where the ground had been disturbed. "Looks like a scuffle maybe. There were certainly a group of them at least."

"Florin," he called to her, catching the clue he'd been looking for out of the corner of his eye. "Here."

She followed his direction, bringing the light over to where he stood looking at something on the floor between crumbling old pews. The light spread across a pair of old boots first, before exposing the fallen body of a very dead man. Even like this, Shilling recognised the man from the wedding.

"Balles," he announced softly.

"He hasn't been dead more than a day," Florin declared, crouching carefully nearer the body and sending more rats scurrying. She inspected his bloodstained chest. "Single penetrative wound. Clean run through. Definitely a sword, but a thin blade — possibly a swordstick? Stabbed from the front too, but no defensive wounds... hm... a group then? He was held by others while another ran him through?"

"Or taken by surprise," Shilling postulated, crouching down and beginning to rifle through the dead man's clothes. "Possibly both."

"Charlie!" Amy rebuked.

"You want to find these diamonds before they make it back to Africa?" he countered, digging through Balles' pockets. He was half-tempted to tell her to check the man's shoes, but the shabby wallet in his coat proved he hadn't been looted already and that didn't bode well. If he hadn't been stripped down, then there was a good chance his killer already had what they wanted from him.

The wallet contained a few small coins, some old ticket stubs, and a little black and white photo. Charlie grimaced when he saw it and kept it away from Florin. The only other item of note was a scrunched letter. It was partially bloodstained but he recognised the signature at the bottom.

"Charlie?" Amy queried. "What is it?"

"A letter from Merrill," he answered reluctantly, scanning his eyes over the short scrawl.

"Can I see?" she asked, scooting closer to him.

He really didn't want to show her, but he couldn't think of a good reason not to. Except… this changed things. This was a truly excellent reason to abandon the case. He had a fairly good idea what had happened now and the smart thing to do would be to hand all evidence to the French police and walk away. He could pay Sterling back. Cut his losses. The curiosity that had been piqued at the wedding was well and truly sated. He'd be happy enough basking in well-founded assumptions for the rest of his life.

But Florin was reading the note over his shoulder.

She was making curious noises. She didn't know what he knew, and he wasn't prepared to tell her. He'd messed up her life enough already. What he really needed to do was get her back home, not drag her into the emotional equivalent of trench warfare. She hung at his shoulder, one hand holding the light for them both, and the other resting lightly on his arm. Her fingers were warm though his sleeve and her soothing perfume was such a gentle relief compared to the odours of their surroundings.

He turned his face slightly to glimpse her expression, telling himself not to do it, but unable to stop. She looked so curious. There was a contemplative crease between her brows. In the golden lamplight, her green eyes and dark skin made her look like a woodland sprite, which was utter nonsense but hauntingly magical. And there was still a dead man on the floor that they hadn't dealt with, so what on earth was he doing staring at Florin when there was work to be done?

She tapped the note tellingly.

> *Monsieur Balles,*
>
> *You can tell Lucille Bonheur that with your collection of this parcel she can consider us even. This pays back my debt and more, and if she ever wants to come after my personal life again, she should watch her step. Speaking of watching one's step, it would be remiss of me not to warn you. If Lucille has fallen in with Argent once more, you are out of your depth. My advice, though of ill-regard to myself, would be to take the jewels and run. Although, I imagine you are as taken with the woman as I once was, and this advice will be heeded as well as I took it myself. She is using you, like she uses everyone, and she and Argent play in a league of their own. The likes of us cannot compete.*
>
> *Consider yourself warned,*
> *Annette Merrill*

"Merrill gave him the diamonds..." Florin

commented, her finger resting on the damning ink. "I bet Sterling would pay to learn that, if nothing else. Now we just have to work out who Argent is. Another acquaintance of Bonheur, of course, but if we ask around…" Florin trailed off, catching sight of Shilling's face and peering at him. "Charlie? Charlie, what's wrong?"

"W-we—" he stuttered and wet his lips before trying again. "We might need to just let this one be, Florin."

"Who is Argent?" she asked, catching on instantly and meeting his eye without flinching.

He kept back his sigh, but he felt his shoulders slump. He would have given anything to dodge the question, but he couldn't lie to her. Not without getting caught in it.

"Marquis Jacques Argent," he answered simply, avoiding anything but the name and title, which already felt like some gross confession. "He's a direct descendant of one of Napoleon I's generals. Owns a large estate outside of Paris."

"And why are you scared of him?" she demanded.

God, that was another horrible question. She was full of awful, piercing questions at the moment. This had all been a terrible idea. He should have left it alone. He should have just let this poor man steal from the rich, to give to the equally rich, while getting murdered, without sticking his nose in it. He was sure Balles had been perfectly capable of getting himself killed in peace without interference. But interfered he had, and now he didn't know how to get out again. The body lay cold at their feet like a solemn reminder.

"You mean aside from the fact that he can have a man killed with such confidence that no repercussion will befall him that he doesn't even bother to dispose of evidence that might implicate him in the murder?" Charlie tried. Florin didn't quite seem to buy it, so he indicated the corpse to emphasise the point.

"That's not the real reason," Florin shook her head. "Look me in the eye, Charlie. Do you have a history with these people?"

"No." That, at least, he could answer honestly.

"Then," she got to her feet and pulled him up with her, "we're going to leave here, we're going to let the police know about the body in the church, and then we're going after the Marquis and the diamonds."

"Why?" Shilling grimaced. "Why can't you just let this one go, Florin?"

"Because you've never left a case unsolved, Charlie," she told him. "Not ever. I'm not going to let you start now just because I'm with you."

He opened his mouth to protest, but that was the exact reason he was trying to run away. Florin, as per usual, had hit the nail bang on the head. If he'd taken the case on his own, he'd be halfway to Argent's estate by now. The thought shut him up and he was left with no argument save the anguished reluctance on his face. Florin stepped close and placed a hand on his cheek. Her touch was so soft and warm it felt like it would melt him. Maybe that was the point.

His breath caught, unwilling to pass his lips when she was potentially close enough to feel it. Everything about the moment reminded him of the kiss in Lord

Pound's office the night they'd caught Harry. The scheme with the lipstick had been genius, but he'd never kissed anyone that way before. He'd never wanted to kiss anyone that way before.

But Amy Florin was different.

She made his throat close up and his heart beat faster and his breath vanish. She maybe even made him want to kiss someone again, with no further agenda than the kiss itself.

"Charlie..." She whispered his name in that informal way she always spoke to him, and he wondered if he was going to have a heart attack. "I don't know what you're scared of, but you don't need to be scared. We can do this. I've got you. Besides, we caught the Jack of Hearts, we're not about to let a few French thieves stop us."

The smile she gave when she said it was impish, heavily dimpled at the corners of her full lips. No sooner were the words spoken then she was turning away again, her hand dropping from his face. The movement was swift and fluid, but the heat of her touch lingered. He could feel it against his face, the delicate trace of her fingers against his throat as her hand had fallen away and brushed ever so lightly against his chest.

His breathing returned as she stepped away, but it didn't come easily and it instantly filled his nose with the unwelcome scent of rot. He missed her perfume and her closeness, but the thought of trying to tell her that filled him with fear. He'd had his words misconstrued before. All his life. Sometimes with disastrous consequences. He couldn't risk that with Florin. Instead, he bottled it and followed her from the ruins.

10

The Argent estate was a sprawling villa. It almost couldn't seem to decide if it was a palace or a castle. Perhaps, over the ages, it had tried to be both. Now, it was a massive section of land with an extensive house that Shilling kept a keen eye on as the carriage brought them up the sweeping, landscaped driveway. He had never been fond of excessive displays of wealth. Actually, he'd never been fond of any displays of wealth. He'd always found wealth of the kind that people liked to display usually meant that someone else was going without. Charlie didn't like to think of people going without.

He made several curious observations regarding the villa as they pulled up. Florin paid the driver for their trip, plus extra to stay a moment in case they were thrown from the front door for daring to come knocking. Shilling insisted they use her father's name to get themselves hospitality here. They might be English, but she was still a Lord's daughter. He had a lot more faith in the concept than she did. However, they needn't have been concerned. In fact, Charlie fast became worried by the ease with which they were admitted.

They were shown to the parlour and set comfortably

to wait with tea and cake, almost reminiscent of Sterling's welcome. But they weren't working for Argent. He had no reason to welcome them this way. Unless...

Charlie's stomach flip-flopped as he sat there and he didn't touch any of the refreshments. His fingers desperately traced the circle of one of his coat buttons and he tried to focus on his breathing to slow his racing heart. He could tell his anxiety was worrying Florin, but there was nothing to be done about that now. He just had to calm his nerves as best he could and wait.

When Argent joined them, he was everything Charlie had expected him to be. The man strode forcefully into the room on long legs, still in his riding tails, removing gloves from his hands as though he had dashed straight in from his horse. He was tall and confident and sickeningly handsome. His skin was darker than stained mahogany and his black hair, barely tinged with grey, was cropped close. He was more than twice their age, but the years were barely noticeable, mostly manifesting in deep laughing crinkles about his eyes. The smile he shot them as he swooped into the room was achingly charming.

"London's boy detective," he grinned as he descended on them. "Your reputation precedes you, *Monsieur* Shilling." He shook Charlie's hand as they stood to greet him, and the glance he shot at Florin turned into a lingering consideration. "And your beautiful lady..."

"My associate is Doctor Florin," Charlie replied coolly.

"*Enchantée*, Doctor," Argent turned, taking her hand gently. Florin clearly hadn't been expecting the same man Shilling had. He felt a faint flicker of panic and guilt as he watched her flush bashfully in the Marquis' company.

"Amelia." She blushed as he kissed her hand. "Amelia Florin."

Argent's lips pressed lingeringly to her fingers for a moment before he unleashed another winning smile at her.

"Amelia..." he tasted her name. "*Magnifique*. A beautiful name for a beautiful woman."

Charlie glared at him. He knew it was just out of fear and not from anything the Marquis had done, but he couldn't help himself. He was worried about Florin, for all that the meeting so far had been perfectly agreeable. Still, Argent caught the look and grinned at him, letting go of Florin's hand and indicating the seats.

"*S'il vous plait*," he invited them. "My house is yours. What brings England's finest investigators to France? Are you chasing another serial killer?" Argent sank into a chair across from them, lounging gracefully with his long legs crossed before him.

Shilling could barely keep his sarcastic accusations in, but he also didn't want to end up like Balles. Better to abandon his natural instincts and play it safe.

"You know us?" he asked instead.

"*Oui*, the saga of your Jack of Hearts made it across the Channel," Argent smiled like they spoke of fiction. "Also, I get some of the English papers. I enjoy reading of your exploits. You are a fascinating man, *Monsieur*

Shilling." Argent eyeballed him appraisingly. "Not what I expected, but it is reputably impossible to catch you on camera."

"I like my privacy," Shilling replied. He knew what Argent meant. People like him expected their opponents to be like them. To be worthy. Adversaries were either of their calibre, or they were not. Argent was tall, regal, affluent, and handsome. Charlie was none of those things.

"Mysterious..." Argent commented, and Charlie definitely felt like the Marquis was teasing him.

"If you'll forgive me prying, my Lord," Florin began cautiously, "we were surprised by your enthusiasm to admit us..."

"It's an honour," Argent smiled. "Celebrity detectives, at my own door? How could I refuse? Your investigation brings you to town, it would be a privilege to host you."

"I find it hard to believe our reputation warrants such generosity..." Florin demurred. She clearly didn't want to do anything to insult their host, but she was also smart enough to know this wasn't everything it appeared. Argent remained unrattled, still smiling his dashing grin.

"Then, *Madame*, you might also find it hard to believe the extent of entertainment my countrymen and I get from the regular tales of the London police having to have their cases solved by a local child." Argent's grin was devastating. Charlie could feel it cut them both from across the room, and he conceded the Marquis' point. Although, he wasn't prepared to be offended by the insult. The people in his life who knew him well all still called him a child on occasion. Argent's dark eyes were as cunning as they were bright, and it was easy to take him at his word. Except, Charlie didn't take men like Argent at their word. Not ever. He wouldn't have trusted the Marquis if the handsome stranger had told him the sky was blue.

"Don't worry, I'm in the process of making the Parisian police look bad too," Charlie admitted, carefully withdrawing Balles' wallet and laying it on the table in front of him. "I find law enforcement globally to be a tool of systematic class oppression. I'm not interested in making them look good anywhere. Which, I suppose, is doing you a favour right now."

"How so?" Argent replied carefully, eyeing the wallet with suspicion but not recognition.

"If I'd left the items I found on the body we discovered in the abandoned Magdalene Church, the police would have connected the dead man to you as quickly as we did, one would hope," he said. "As it stands, I anticipate them being half a week behind us. *Monsieur* Balles was not a man without enemies, after all."

"He was not," Argent agreed, settling again. He linked his fingers and relaxed in a way that set Shilling's teeth on edge. Charlie despised the thought of someone who could be so certain of their power that a confrontation with evidence implicating them in murder was easily dismissed.

"You don't seem surprised to learn of his death..." Florin pointed out.

"I'm not," Argent shrugged. "I met the man once and it was not an experience I would care to repeat. As you say, *Monsieur* Shilling, Balles was not a man without enemies. His untimely death was inevitable."

"And your involvement in it?" Shilling challenged, forgetting himself and his company for a moment.

"*Quoi?*" Argent shrugged. "I'm sure I don't know what you mean."

"We have evidence to suggest otherwise," Florin countered. "Lord Argent, we mean no disrespect, but we were hired by an English noblewoman who was robbed by Mister Balles to recover her stolen possessions, which we believe have come into your hands. While I can also believe that you didn't know the items in question were stolen, we are going to need to take them back."

Shilling barely contained a scathing huff. He, personally, meant every disrespect and was utterly confident that Argent knew very well that he had acquired stolen property. Argent was still smiling at them like he found them delightfully entertaining and was by no means even remotely threatened by their accusations. When he spoke again, he leant against the arm of his chair to bring his attention closer to Florin.

"Your grace of character does you credit, Doctor Florin," he praised her diplomacy. "But if your only reason for visiting is in pursuit of an unexplained parcel of diamonds… I'm sorry to disappoint you. They are not here."

"I find that very hard to believe," Shilling replied.

"Just because I know what Balles was supposed to

be carrying doesn't mean I found it," Argent countered. "For your enchanting Doctor, *Monsieur* Shilling, I could even have been prevailed upon to return the stolen treasure, but the diamonds were not on *Monsieur* Balles' person when my people went to meet him. I don't know what he did with them, but I do not have them."

"Is that why you still have Lucille Bonheur locked in a tower upstairs?" Charlie demanded, unable to stop himself.

The room froze and he could sense Florin holding her breath as she stared shocked daggers at him. He had the decency to feel guilty about that. Even Argent's eyes narrowed and his smile finally slipped. He gave Shilling a considered perusal.

"Sorry, you probably know her better as Viviane, correct?" Charlie pushed, not prepared to give up his one victory in the room. "Viviane... uh—?"

"Argent," the Marquis finished cuttingly. "Viviane Argent. My wife."

Even Charlie was forced to bite his tongue at that point. He could feel Florin's daggers staring sharper into the side of his face. Argent's congeniality faded and a notable bitter twist haunted his lips.

"You may know her by a dozen different names, *Monsieur* Shilling," he sneered. "But to me she is Viviane Argent. We were never legally separated, despite, I'm sure, her marriages to many other men before and after me under different aliases."

"Wife or not, you can't keep her locked in a tower," Shilling insisted.

"You are welcome to stay in my house, *Monsieur*, but

don't make the mistake of thinking my marriage has anything to do with you," Argent warned. He tapped his fingers against the arm of his chair, still regarding Shilling with a sharp consideration. "And what name do you know her by?"

"I don't," Shilling lied, feeling himself flush with the mistruth of it and attempting to balance it with a fact. "I've never met her."

Argent eyed him up. The Marquis clearly wasn't sure if he should believe him or not.

"Given that this all seems connected, I would quite like the opportunity to speak to her," Charlie tried hopefully.

"That isn't going to happen," Argent shut him down.

"But she started this," Shilling insisted. "She did, didn't she? She organised for Balles to steal those diamonds, to pay you, to buy her freedom? I'm right."

"I'm sure you're very clever, *Monsieur* Shilling," Argent sighed, standing up.

"You're after revenge, Lord Argent, but you'll never have it," Charlie warned. "It doesn't matter how long you hold her, or what you make her steal for you, you'll never recover what she stole from you. You'll never recover what you lost."

Argent paused by the arm of his chair. He was no longer meeting their eyes, and the entertainment they had initially provided was clearly wearing thin, but it had not entirely evaporated.

"*Monsieur* Shilling, you and Doctor Florin are welcome to stay the night. Explore the grounds, take a walk down to the village — I'm sure you will find it perfectly... quaint. If you are here for the diamonds, I am sorry to waste your time. If you're here for Viviane..." he looked up and met Shilling's eye with exactly the ruthless warning Charlie had been expecting when they arrived. "Tell the English that if they want their pound of flesh, they have to get in line."

"If you're keeping a woman imprisoned against her will, after murdering her lover, the police will be interested to hear about it," Shilling threatened.

Argent smirked as he sauntered towards the door without looking back and called, "If you had anything worth taking to the police, you would have done it already."

Charlie glared. Argent clearly knew his politics, even more so than Shilling had unwittingly voiced. He wasn't going to law enforcement unless he was in immediate danger, which the Marquis seemed to have no interest in inflicting. Argent had nothing against the amusing British sleuths. After all, to him they were nothing more than humorous children.

"Oh," he stopped in the doorway and looked back at them. "One room or two?" He was definitely teasing now. The mirth of earlier had returned to his expression and he regarded them with mischievous eyes. Charlie wasn't really surprised to find the Marquis twisting the dagger on them at the end. He had maintained the upper hand, and he wanted to make damn sure they knew it would stay that way.

"*Deux. Merci,*" Charlie replied, meeting his eye unflinchingly.

Argent laughed and graced them with his most

insinuating smirk yet, before striding from the room.

Shilling sat like a statue in his chair, cold with indignation. He *knew* Argent was behind this. He knew Bonheur must have inadvertently fallen into his clutches and then done whatever was in her power to buy her freedom, but after the stunt she had pulled all those years ago, robbing him and running out on him, her freedom would come at a steep price. The diamonds should have covered it, so she would have conned Balles into getting them for her. Somewhere along the line, there had been a hiccup in the plan. He just had to work out what.

In the meantime, he had dragged Florin into the last place he'd ever want to put her. Well, not quite the last… in prison with Harry was probably the last place he'd want her. Or in the mouth of an active volcano. Or on a ship in a typhoon. Or— no. The important thing was that this wasn't a good place for her, even if there were worse places. She was sitting at his side, hands clasped and face flaming at the implication they shared a room. He didn't blame her.

"How did you know Bonheur was here?" she asked softly, once one of them regained the confidence to speak.

"Bars on the tower window," Shilling muttered. "I saw them when we were driving in. They haven't been there long enough to age or rust too badly. The only reason to put them up there is to keep someone imprisoned in the room."

"And you guessed it was Bonheur?" Florin checked.

"Seemed the safest deduction," he shrugged.

"Anyone else, anyone Argent cared for less, could be thrown in a regular dungeon. She was his wife. Part of him still loves her. It wouldn't hurt so much if he didn't."

"And you think she's trying to buy her freedom?" Florin murmured.

"It's the only thing that makes sense," Charlie sighed, pushing himself wearily to his feet. He rubbed his face and scrunched his hair, trying to work out some of his frustration. Florin watched him curiously and he wished he had more answers for her. "I'm sorry I dragged you into this," he apologised.

"You didn't drag me anywhere, Charlie," she sighed, standing primly and approaching him. "And the only thing you have been dragging is your feet." She tugged his hands from his face and gently set about straightening his hair with light fingers. It wasn't going to do much good, but it was better than nothing. He stood stiffly, heart in his throat, as she lingered close, her hands running through his messy straw hair. The faint lavender in her perfume seemed to be losing the soothing qualities he had come to associate with it, or he was becoming easier to agitate.

"Do you believe him about the diamonds?" Florin whispered near his ear as she let him go.

There was no one else in the room, but he appreciated her discretion. A small smile tugged the corner of his crooked lips and his eyes softened with admiration.

"You don't?" he countered, his pride in her more audible than his words.

Florin gave him a reproachful look that triggered his own smug smirk. God, she was brilliant. She was so sharp he could kiss her, but that would be wildly inappropriate, and he didn't much feel like getting cut by her edges. There was too much in her face that reminded him of the present danger they were still in.

"If Balles had been empty-handed they would have interrogated him or kidnapped him, not killed him," Florin murmured. "At the very least they would have searched his body, and I do not believe they would have bothered to redress him for us afterwards."

"Agreed," Shilling smiled.

"Also," she added carefully with a furtive glance at the room, "Argent is left-handed. Balles was run through by someone angling a blade with their left hand. That is by no means a certainty, but if I was meeting my ex-wife's current lover in a clandestine blackmail drop, I would probably murder him once he handed over the treasure too."

"You wouldn't kill anyone, Florin," Charlie assured her loyally.

"Try me," she warned him. Her tone was threatening, yet goading, and he knew she didn't mean it. The playfulness of it made him smile.

Made him yearn.

Yearning was not something Charlie was familiar with. Not with regards to another person. He didn't know what to do except stand there and blush, and remember the way Argent had looked at them when he'd asked if they shared a room, and then blush harder.

"For now, I think we should assume he was lying…"

Florin proposed, either oblivious or kindly ignoring his embarrassment. She linked her arm in his as though readying to leave the room.

"Of course," Charlie breathed. "But where does that leave us?"

"Snooping," she smiled. "Argent said we were welcome to stay, welcome to investigate the grounds and the village, so we do just that. Surely there will people around willing to part with information."

"We need to be careful, Florin," he warned her. "There's a difference between Argent knowing that we will snoop and having him catch us snooping."

"Of course," she agreed, guiding him from the parlour. "But if Jacques Argent killed Philippe Balles and stole those diamonds, I guarantee at least one person in his service knows."

11

They decided their best course of action would be to split up. Amy was certain she would have better luck talking to the women of the house without Charlie. He was an observational genius, bless him, but he wasn't always good with people. He was the first to agree. She sent him off to investigate to the best of his talents, while she set about finding someone to gossip with. This produced the unfortunate dilemma of needing to gain the trust of someone who should not, for the sake of their own best interests, trust her. It also meant she was probably going to have to do something regrettable to provoke an incident in which someone might confide in her.

This started with a misplaced broom in the corridor while two of the maids were having a smoke break. It was very carefully misplaced. Amy didn't actually want to hurt anyone. Well, not badly. It was too perfect an opportunity to pass up.

She set it so that someone would trip just outside the open door of her assigned room. Part of her felt a faint stir of suspicion that Charlie would deeply disapprove of this plan if he knew about it. Good thing they had separated. He was intensely protective of servants.

When the woman tripped and went crashing to her knees outside the room, Amy certainly felt a strong rush of guilt. The maid cried out as the broom caught her ankle and she tumbled, her friend failing to catch her as she fell. Amy heard the cry and the thump and rushed to help. Initially, the women tried to wave her away, but she insisted, informing them that she was a doctor.

With the maid's somewhat reluctant blessing, Amy checked her over. The woman had rolled her ankle when she had tripped and fallen on her knees. It would hurt a bit, but nothing was really injured. It would be easy enough to walk off within the hour. She passed that along as best she could, her French stuttering slightly with nerves. Fortunately, the maids seemed to find the stammering, well-meaning, English doctor entertaining. They were smiling at her, at least.

"How long have you been working here?" she asked, in her uncertain French.

The fallen woman had been here for three years, her companion for five. Amy commented on the length of time. It was, after all, a decent length of time for young women to stay gathering experience in one household.

"It's a good place to work, and very convenient for anyone from the village," the younger one informed her.

"The work can be a bit harder than some of the smaller houses in the area, but at least here the Master never shops at home," the other commented. "Marquis Argent is a gentleman. You don't have to worry about getting harassed here."

Amy gave them a considered nod. That was good to

hear, and mildly surprising given the image of him Charlie had been building in her mind. The Lord of the Manor was handsome and charming, the kind of man she had assumed would take anything he wanted, including his staff.

"I hadn't expected such loyalty to his wife," she replied carefully, hoping her French didn't betray her. "Not after the stories I'd heard."

"He's not loyal to her," one of the women scoffed scandalously. "Lady Argent was a con-woman who robbed him and vanished twenty years ago. Everyone knows about it. The scandal was devastating. Lord Argent never recovered from it, but he owes her nothing. He famously frequents the High Houses of Paris."

"Even now that he's got her back?" Amy asked curiously.

The maids looked at her in confusion. Bollocks. Apparently the tower guest was a secret. Of course. If you were keeping a kidnapped woman locked up against her will, only the essential few would know.

"*Je suis désolé*," Amy apologised. "I'd just heard…"

"He went to Paris the other night," the older maid shrugged.

"*Oui*," her companion agreed. "Night before last. Took his guards, stayed the single night, came back. If that isn't the sign of a High House visit, I don't know what is."

Amy held her tongue and gave them a conceding nod, adding a small airheaded flourish as though, silly her, she had completely misunderstood an earlier comment. Her French just wasn't as good as it should be. Internally, her mind heard the clunk of a damning cell door. That was proof that Argent had been away in Paris the night Balles had been killed. He could have done it.

Before she could ask anything else, footsteps approached, and the old housekeeper came shuffling purposefully into view. She immediately began berating the maids on the floor, who tried to explain the incident with the fall in return. The speed with which they conversed made it difficult for Amy to follow, but she tried to intercede on the maids' behalf. After all, it wasn't their fault.

Still, as she tried to explain to the old woman that there had been an accident and she was helping, the blood drained out of the housekeeper's face. She stared at Amy like she had seen a ghost.

"I'm Doctor Florin," she tried to explain. "My partner and I are visiting while we investigate a case for an English Lady."

"*Elle t'a amené ici!*" the woman cried like an accusation.

"Uh…" Amy paused. Something had been lost or misconstrued in translation. The housekeeper said someone had brought her here. A woman. In actuality, Charlie had brought her here, but supposedly it was at the behest of Lady Sterling. How this woman knew Sterling or anything to do with her was a mystery. "No I, uh, I'm here with the detective. The British detective, Mister Shilling…?" She tried to make her point in French, but she knew it was still broken and halting.

The housekeeper ushered the maids up off the floor and stood protectively in front of them. Amy abandoned her interrogation. She didn't know what she'd done wrong, but something had clearly spooked the older woman. Besides, she already knew enough from the maids. Perhaps the next port of call would be a conversation with Argent's guards — especially any who had travelled with him.

The housekeeper was still staring at her. She clutched at her breast and muttered something Amy didn't understand. Perhaps some prayer. She thought she could make out '*mère*' for mother. Possibly great mother or holy mother. She wasn't sure. The other maids clearly did understand, because they startled at the words and looked at Amy like she'd suddenly turned into a bear.

That just made everything all the more confusing, and rather humiliating. She apologised repeatedly, to the best of her ability, as she hurried away, still completely baffled as to what she might have done, but no one looked in the mood to explain her transgression. Hopefully she would have better luck with the guards.

Shilling had weighed up his options and, as per usual, gone with the one that interested him the most, regardless of the danger. When he finished sneaking to the top of the tower, he found the door locked but unguarded. Either that meant Argent trusted his chains and bars to hold, or he didn't trust his guards not to be tricked by his wife. Possibly both.

Either way, Charlie was grateful as he knelt by the lock and set to picking it. The tumblers weren't complicated. He slid the pins in carefully and was done in under five seconds. Not a record, but fast enough to make him smile. After all, lockpicking was merely a hobby. He'd never claim it as a career skill.

He opened the door cautiously and snuck inside. The room's occupant was waiting for him. She sat on the single bed along one side of the room, and sure enough a shackle around her ankle kept her chained to it. The room was simply furnished, clean and tidy, but the light through the window was streaked with the shadows of the bars. It wasn't a bad prison, but it was still a prison.

Shilling stood with his back pressed to the door. The woman on the bed sat politely with a book in her lap. Her red hair was streaked with so much white it was beginning to look blonde. Beneath a scattering of dark freckles, deep lines from many lives were starting to etch themselves upon her skin. Her eyes were shrewd and curious, and the green severity in them when they pierced him was achingly familiar.

"*Bonjour, Madame* Argent," he greeted her, still holding himself tightly by the door.

"*Bonjour...*" she replied, clearly curious, before pointing out that of all the people she was expecting, he was none of them.

"No," he agreed, switching to English. "But the Marquis wouldn't have needed to pick the lock, and

Philippe Balles is dead. I don't know who else you might have been expecting. My name is Charles Shilling, and I have a few questions regarding Jacques Argent, Philippe Balles, Annette Merrill, and Lady Olive Sterling — particularly regarding some stolen diamonds."

Lucille Bonheur, also known as Viviane Argent, rested her head back against the wall with a smile that was almost a breath of laughter.

"The boy detective..." she smiled softly at him; all trace of her French accent withdrawn. "I've heard of you. I'm surprised to find you here. You're... shorter than I expected."

"I was hired to investigate," he told her politely, ignoring her comment. He was never anything anyone expected.

"Then God help anyone who stands in your way," she smiled grimly. Her severe eyes measured him up. "Your infamy in obsession and success is matched only by the infamy of your politics, Mister Charles Shilling."

"My infamy pales in comparison to your own, Miss Elizabeth Florin," he replied, an unfamiliar darkness settling on his tongue at the use of one of her old names. He immediately decided he didn't like using the name 'Florin' for the woman before him. She glowered at him.

"Of course," she sneered. "I knew as soon as I saw you start popping up in the papers, eventually that Pound bastard would hire you."

"I'm not presently working for Henry Pound," Charlie assured her. "I was hired by Lady Sterling to recover the diamonds your associate Balles stole from

Merrill's wedding to buy your freedom from Argent." He paused and looked around the room. "How's that working out?"

"Don't insult me, boy," she sneered.

Charlie cocked his head to the side in consideration and regarded her. Her reaction had been fair. They both knew Argent had killed Balles and kept the diamonds, declaring them insufficient payment for property stolen. The poor man had no idea. Although, Charlie was wavering on how sorry he could feel for him. Argent wasn't exactly a saint.

Lucille was still weighing him with her eyes. In a different face he would have been undone by those eyes, but there was too much cruelty in her look, however unintended.

"Mister Shilling," Lucille sighed, "you and I both know Jacques has those diamonds and that I have no power over his possession of them. Why are you bothering with me?"

He pursed his lips thoughtfully, head still cocked.

"I'm looking for a reason to help you," he admitted. "But… I'm not sure you deserve it." His eyes scoured the room again. It was hard to say that to a woman sitting in chains. Imprisonment was not rehabilitation, but he would concede that Lucille Bonheur was possibly beyond rehabilitation, and at least here she was forced to refrain from pursuing any future victims. At some point one had to concede that actions had consequences, and Lucille's consequences had caught up with her.

"Fascinating," she commented gently, almost

smiling at him again.

Charlie knew that look. He'd seen it in the eyes of a lot of people before. That was the look his opponents gave him when they thought they saw a soft spot. It was the way Argent had looked at him earlier. It was the look a fox gave a rabbit. Charlie was many things, but he was never a rabbit. Too many people realised that too late.

Lucille spoke delicately. "I would have thought, Mister Shilling, that a man of your leanings would understand me better than anyone. Your sympathies are rather well… scandalised."

A normal person would have said 'documented', and Shilling resisted the urge to roll his eyes. The Florin he knew would have found this woman conceited. He rather hoped, perhaps even prayed, they would never meet.

"Redistributing wealth to erase poverty is not the same as stealing from the rich to make oneself rich," he replied coolly.

"I'm erasing my own poverty," she retorted.

"No," Charlie shook his head. "There is a line between bettering your conditions and hurting others to sustain your compulsion. You could have stopped so many times… but you don't. You always have to bleed people until you get bored. Tricking people is what you enjoy. It's a game to you, and money is just how you keep score."

"Money is freedom, and I like my freedom," Lucille countered. "I shouldn't have to be tethered to a wealthy lover just to buy bread."

"But you hurt people to do it," he argued. "We're not talking about money you take from those who don't need it to help those who do. You deliberately leave victims. You wouldn't be in your current predicament if you didn't."

"What do you care, boy detective?" she huffed. "Rumour has it you loathe the bourgeoisie as much as anyone. Why do you care if I bring them down a notch?"

"Because you abandoned her," he answered simply, knowing the problem and his issues ran deeper than that, and yet equally knowing he couldn't venture to those deeper levels until he had crossed this bridge. This personal and painful bridge. It didn't seem right that it should hurt him, but somehow it did. She knew instantly what he was talking about and the silence sat between them like fire, growing bigger and hotter and brighter until Lucille couldn't stand it.

"I didn't know," she muttered finally. "When I left Jacques, I didn't know I was pregnant. I... I might not have left if I'd known. You have to understand, for all that he is rich and handsome, Jacques Argent is controlling and cruel."

"I believe you," Shilling nodded. He did believe that. He understood wholeheartedly that Argent would not have been a good husband. He would have tried, but Shilling could easily imagine how those two would have brought out the worst in each other. It would be very hard to trust with a wife like Viviane Argent. The Marquis would have been smart enough to know something was wrong, even if he didn't realise he was getting played. It would have ended badly.

"I didn't know how fragile David was," Lucille defended. "I'd already moved on to him when I realised I was carrying a child. I wasn't certain… not until she was born…" Lucille pressed her lips together as she trailed off and turned her face to the window, gazing out through the bars. For a brief moment, Shilling saw a genuine flicker of pain in her expression before her natural hardness settled in again and she turned back to him. "I thought it would work out with David. He was gentle, but when the baby was Jacques' I knew I had been found out. The Pounds would not have kept me. I fled before they could throw me out." Lucille took a pained breath and her nostrils flared. "You can't criticise me, boy. I left my baby in the lap of luxury, betrothed to a future Lord —"

"Who turned out to be serial killer," Shilling couldn't help but interject.

"No one knew that then!" she snapped. "The boy wasn't even walking when I left. How was I to know that the son of the Lord Chief Justice was going to grow up to be a monster?! Even you took months to catch him!" Lucille huffed indignantly, trying to calm her temper. "Do not mistake the speed of my decision for ease, boy. I left my baby girl in a much better state than my own situation when she was born. Pound wouldn't have turned out a baby over her mother's indiscretions. She would want for nothing —"

"Except a mother," Charlie retorted, interrupting again.

Lucille gave him a curious look. He constantly felt

like she was trying to calculate his workings. That could be where his Florin got it from. But Lucille didn't know him. It wasn't the same.

"Mister Shilling…" the woman across the room almost purred. "Are you in love with my Amelia?"

"No," Charlie answered politely, shaking his head.

"Then why do you care?" Lucille pressed. "I know you know her. I saw that she helped you catch Henry Junior. You stand at my jail cell, grilling me about a daughter I never met, and you want me to believe it's not because you're soft on her?"

Shilling considered this. He was soft on her. Florin was his friend. A good friend. He cared very deeply for her. Was that love? Quite. But was it the kind of love Lucille meant?

"I've never been in love before," he admitted softly, stepping away from the door and crossing to the window. "Not the kind you're referring to. I don't know if that is the appropriate term for what I feel, but Doctor Florin is a dear friend, and I do care for her."

"Ah. You're one of those types," Lucille commented.

"I don't know what that means," Charlie shrugged, not much caring what she meant either. He peered out the window at the picturesque landscape beyond. "I have been dreading this trip. I was loath to put her in the firing line of you or the Marquis. I don't want to give either of you the opportunity to hurt her."

"She's here?!" Lucille gasped.

"She wanted to work the case with me," Charlie sighed. "I didn't know it would lead us here, and once I realised my mistake, I couldn't drag her away without telling her the truth. It was not my truth to share."

"Jacques has met her?!" Lucille demanded.

"He didn't recognise her," Shilling assured. "He has no reason to. He never caught you as Florin, so he wouldn't know there was a daughter carrying the name."

"How did you catch me?" she asked. "No one else ever did."

"I was just curious," Charlie shrugged at the scenery. "I heard the story about Henry Pound's daughter years ago, and when I started official investigative work, I had to get his blessing to work with law enforcement. My first big case came through him five years ago. After that, I looked into you a little, between jobs, just in case. Figured if he ever did decide he wanted to find you, it would help to know where you were." He turned to face her again, leaning nonchalantly against the windowsill and grimacing in a way that exacerbated the crooked line of his mouth. "You weren't that hard to trace."

Lady Argent gave him the darkest, most unimpressed look she could muster. "You should tell that to the sixty-three minor European nobles chasing me," she muttered.

"Fifty-seven, actually, some of your old marks are no longer with us," he replied. "Also, I rather think you wouldn't want me to, given that your life will be easier if they're not on your heels."

"Does that mean you're going to get me out of here?" she asked, unable to suppress the hope.

"I think I rather ought to," Shilling sighed. "You are

Florin's mother, after all. However, if I help you, there are conditions."

"Of course there are…" she drawled.

"The first is that you help me obtain the diamonds from Argent so that I can complete my case," he insisted.

"Disappointing, but fair," Lucille conceded.

"The second is that we keep Florin safe at all costs," he said. "I don't want her getting anymore tangled up in this than she already is." He gave the woman before him a grave look. "You and I have done enough to damage her life. She isn't allowed to know who you really are. She isn't allowed to know who you and Argent are to her. I don't want to force that emotional baggage on her."

"Don't you think she deserves to know?" Lucille challenged.

"What she deserves is a long, peaceful, and gentle life," he replied. "Unfortunately, you abandoned her at birth to an engagement with Harry Pound and then she befriended me. Now, we simply have to do the best we can with what we've got."

Lucille smiled at him, a much softer smile than any other she had shown him. The hard edge in her familiar green eyes diluted to near nonexistence.

"You are in love with her…" she commented softly. Charlie ignored that.

"The third condition," he continued, "is to please at least consider how easy it will be for me to find you and bring you under the arm of the law if you continue your destructive behaviour."

"I thought you didn't believe in incarceration," she teased him, and in that moment he could see exactly where Amy got her talent for banter from.

"I think it is used far too liberally to oppress the poor and as a means for the wealthy to bury troubles of inequality, instead of addressing the issues caused by their heinous system," he answered honestly. "Still, I will concede that there are those, like Harry Pound, where I simply have no other solutions to offer in order to protect them and others." He gave her a serious look. "I would hate, Lady Argent, to break you from so beautiful a prison, only to have to drop you in a worse one."

She glowered again. "I take your point, Mister Shilling," she sighed. "Very well, I agree to your terms."

She agreed far too quickly, and Shilling was of half a mind to just leave her there. But he wasn't going to, even if he knew she would try and play him. At least she wasn't really being subtle about it. He took his lockpicks and approached the bed carefully, as though nearing a viper. She was smart enough not to attack the help though.

He heard the footsteps too late. He was still kneeling by the bed, picking the lock on Lucille's shackle, when the door burst open. Shilling leapt to his feet, dodging the blow that came his way. The blade swung back. He froze as the point of the sword against his chest pinned him against the barred window. Jacques Argent glared at him with murderous intent, pressing the tip of his blade to Charlie's shirt. Shilling stood with his hands raised, trying to think of something he could say to defend himself.

"Looks like you've outstayed your welcome already, *Monsieur* Shilling…" the Marquis growled.

12

A group of Argent's personal guards were gathered in the back courtyard near the stables. They were drinking and sparring with an enthusiasm that suggested to Amy that they were mercenaries. Unless Argent gave his staff a long and casual leash. The maids certainly thought well of him, insomuch as she had been able to garner an opinion before they fled from her.

The behaviour had been so unusual that she approached her next targets with a great deal more caution and utterly no deception. Besides, the guards were all armed. They were all trained in the use of their swords. Some of them even carried pistols on their belts like they fancied themselves American cowboys.

They saw her coming across the way, and she held herself with dignity as a few less discreet members nudged each other and pointed. She took their curiosity of her as permission to loiter and watch. However, it didn't take long for the curiosity to become pointed.

One of the guards drifted nearer, eyeing her up severely. The woman was tall, with darker skin than Amy, and her command felt absolute, even in her walk. Almost certainly the captain of this band. She inquired what Amy was doing there, but the naturally demanding tone was softened by genuine interest.

Amy replied that she was just looking, and not for trouble, but something in her voice must have given her away, because even more people turned to regard her when she spoke.

"You're English…?" the Captain checked, eyes narrowing.

"*Oui,*" she confirmed. "Doctor Florin, from London. My partner and I are guests of the Marquis. I work with an English detective, Mister Shilling, whom Marquis Argent is familiar with…"

The Captain threw a look back over her shoulder at the other guards. They were all beginning to pay attention now, as though something far more interesting than their self-made entertainment was occurring. Amy held herself cautiously. This felt like a trap, but she couldn't imagine why. She had guest rights, and the air of her inquisitors was not aggressive, but she didn't like the intensity of their interest.

"And what, pray, does Marquis Argent have English detectives investigating?" the Captain asked.

"I'm afraid we're visiting the Marquis, not working for him," Amy replied. "We're investigating for an Englishwoman, looking into the disappearance of one Phillippe Balles." She watched them carefully as she said it, searching for any hint of rising defence or guilt.

She got the opposite.

A few sly expressions and smug glances were shared amongst the guards. The Captain herself was smiling as she eyed Amy up again. She turned slowly and stalked back towards her crew with an inviting stride that bid

Amy follow. They reached the table with the wine that stood next to the sparring area, and the tall woman ran a finger down the centre of a sword resting on the table.

"Do you fence, Doctor?" she taunted, lightly flicking up the blade and holding it out. "If you can beat me, I'll tell you where Balles is."

The other guards began to laugh and jeer. Amy didn't flinch. She took the offered rapier by the handle, and gave it an expert twirling flick to test it. The point of her blade stopped just short of the Captain's chin, and shut their audience up.

"I can fence," Amy assured, aware that the words were unrequired at this point. "And Balles' body was in the ruins of the Magdalene Church, until we brought it to the attention of the police back in Paris."

The guards renewed their hollering with extra vigour, watching Amy challenge their leader. The Captain took up her own sword with an impressed smile. She teased her blade along Amy's as the two readied themselves to begin. The aim seemed, from what Amy had deduced earlier, to be simply to disarm each other. No one was dressed to avoid injury, but no one was striking to injure either. She hoped she was included under those rules, although she wasn't wholly sure why the guards were so quick to include her in their fun.

"Then we duel for the identity of the murderer?" the Captain jested.

"A full confession?" Amy asked, moving quickly to strike. The taller woman blocked her easily, parrying her strokes and fending her off. Amy's confidence wavered as she realised that the Captain was unsurprisingly much better than her.

"It won't do you much good," the Captain grinned, twirling away and standing ready, arms out and blade before her, waiting to catch Amy when she struck. "By the time the law gets involved, it's just your word against mine."

Amy tried to decipher a way out of this mess. She couldn't win the fight. The Captain was just playing with her, taunting her like she was a child in training. However, there was something telling about the Captain's style. It helped with the case, if not the current predicament.

Amy lunged to attack. She'd never really gotten the hang of feinting, but the Captain knew how. She gave Amy a short rally, parrying her blade easily, but with a satisfying series of clangs that made it sound like she was doing better than she was. Then came the feint. Amy fell for it completely, moving right and almost falling as the Captain dodged around her, playfully smacking her behind with the flat of her blade. Amy yelped as she was lightly spanked and the guards laughed.

She should have felt humiliated, but she was too confounded by the behaviour. She turned on the grinning Captain, who danced patiently behind her, light on her toes, and waited for Amy to ready herself again. Perhaps this was simply fun at her expense, but it didn't feel like it. She felt as though the Captain was trying to treat her as a friend — as someone who belonged and could be included in the team's camaraderie, even if she wasn't really good enough to compete.

Half of her wanted to toss down her sword and call it a day. It wasn't a fight she could win. Her hair was coming loose and dark red ringlets were escaping around her face and getting in her eyes. Sweat was starting to stick them to her neck and cheeks. This was not easy work in a full dress and skirts. Not when her competition was twice her age, multiple times her skill and experience, and moving casually in a neat uniform of shirt, vest, and trousers. Still, quitting wasn't in her vocabulary.

She eyed the Captain carefully, evaluating her footwork. Then she moved to strike. It was close, much closer than anything else had been. She was met with a quick parry and moved just as quickly again, stepping forward to meet the Captain's blow and counter it. It could almost have worked, but the Captain struck against her blade in quick succession, jolting up her arm. The swords slid together with a steely rasp as both women pushed against each other. Then the Captain hooked her hilt in Amy's and pulled away, ripping the sword from her grasp.

Amy yelped as her weapon was torn from her fingers and launched through the air. The Captain bounced back gracefully, catching the hilt in her free hand, and standing at ease with both weapons. Amy sighed bitterly and shook her head, but more in disappointment at herself. She conceded the defeat graciously. Besides, she had known it was coming.

"I'm afraid I have nothing to tell you after all,

Doctor," the Captain smiled gently.

"You don't have to tell me anything," Amy sighed, rubbing her hand where the hilt had banged her on its way out. "You're right handed. Balles was killed by left handed attacker, like Jacques Argent." She stared the Captain down coolly. "I know Argent killed Balles and stole those diamonds. I know you lot were there. Even if you won't confirm it, science will prove I'm right."

Now the guards were paying attention. It had been foolish, proud. She shouldn't have challenged them like that, but perhaps she was more of a sore loser than she realised. Maybe it had just been such a long time since she'd had a win, and these days it often felt like she'd already lost everything. The Captain still stood at ease, and her stance wasn't threatening, even if her smile was gone. There was a dark glower about her eyes now.

"So you're here for her..." the Captain sighed. "I should have known. Your mother sent for you, no?"

"No," Amy scoffed. "No one sent for me. I don't have a mother."

The Captain flicked a quick glance at her guards. They all looked surprised at that. Amy searched them with her eyes. She didn't understand what was going on.

"Everyone has a mother," the Captain replied.

"Well, obviously," Amy muttered. "But I've never met mine. She abandoned me at birth. I was adopted and raised by Lord Henry Pound — my father—" Amy snatched the sword back from the Captain, startling the other woman as she raised the blade again "—who made sure I knew how to defend myself."

A few of the guards had jumped at her sudden feat of resistance, but the Captain stayed calm and collected in the face of adversary. Amy held her blade at the ready, but the Captain did not raise her sword to meet it. She stood and looked down on Amy with grave consideration. Her free hand came up and rubbed her mouth thoughtfully.

"You believe this…?" she inquired.

Amy lowered her sword. If this was a trick, she was prepared to fall for it. Believe what? It was the truth. She hadn't said anything that didn't make sense, that was what the French were for. The Captain must have deduced something from her expression, because the tall woman shook her head ruefully with a sigh.

"This… Lord Pound," she said. "This Englishman. He is not your father…"

Charlie could feel the windowsill digging into his back as he pressed himself hard against it, trying to escape Argent's blade. The tip of the sword pressed against his chest and he held his breath, praying he wasn't about to be skewered.

"Looks like you've outstayed your welcome already, *Monsieur* Shilling…" the Marquis growled. "Or whatever your real name is."

"My name is Shilling," Charlie wheezed, pressing himself as firmly as he could to the window. "I didn't lie to you."

"You expect me to believe that?" Argent sneered. "No one knows what Charles Shilling looks like — you could be anyone. Another of my wife's many scurrying minions. I should never have fallen for such an outlandish tale. Viviane, I always knew there would be a backup plan to that useless mule in the church."

"I'm no one's back up plan," Charlie insisted breathlessly, starting to feel like he was going to turn blue.

"For God's sake, Jacques!" Lucille exclaimed. "The boy is exactly who he says he is! This isn't a plot! You've read about London's boy detective; you know he's an anarchist! He's not here for me personally, he just doesn't believe in incarceration!"

"Does he believe in death?" Argent asked, lifting his blade to Charlie's throat.

Charlie did believe in death. He'd seen a lot of it. He wasn't sure it was a question he was supposed to answer though. The sword to his throat made it impossible to speak, so the postulation had to be rhetorical. Surely.

"You can't kill him, Jacques!" Lucille ordered. "He's here with Amelia, you can't hurt him!"

"So you do know them," Argent snarled.

"It's not what you think!" Lucille begged, and Charlie didn't blame her for failing to elaborate further. That could have been even more deadly. "Please, Jacques, just let the boy go!"

"Why the concern, Viviane?" Argent taunted. "He's not yours, is he?" The Marquis eyed Shilling up and down. "He doesn't look like yours."

"Not me," Charlie whispered, meeting Argent's eye with damning seriousness. Argent must have seen something in his look, because the sword dropped an inch from Charlie's throat. Not far enough to feel safe, but enough that he could breathe properly. He lifted his hand to his neck and rubbed his skin nervously, but he didn't break eye contact with the Marquis. "I meant what I said downstairs, Lord Argent. This is pointless. Keeping your wife locked up in here? Perhaps there is a sense of justice, a cold and bitter vengeance, at punishing her for what she did, at hurting her as she hurt you... but surely you want to be better than that? If not for yourself... for... for whomever may care about the two of you. There is no point keeping her here until she has paid back what she took from you, that... that's impossible. No one can ever, *ever*, replace what you lost that day..." Charlie trailed off, listening to the footsteps pounding on the stairs outside the room. He really hoped he hadn't said too much, but Argent was looking at him like realisation was suddenly dawning, and it was the dawn of an apocalypse.

"STOP!" a familiar voice yelled. Amy burst through the doorway, sword raised and pointed at Argent. She held the blade like she knew how to use it, levelled at the Marquis and her eyes measured him down the gleaming steel. Her skirts were bundled in her other hand, and her auburn curls were coming loose and unkempt around her face. Her cheeks were flushed, face glistening with sweat, and she was breathing like she'd sprinted the entire way up the tower.

The image Charlie had conjured of her once as some

wild fae sprite came roaring back to his conscious, and he was suddenly reminded of the last time she had burst into a room like this to save him. Maybe he really did need to start taking more care with his cases, if only so that she didn't think he constantly needed to be rescued. Her present beauty was radiant and feral, but standing between the Marquis and his wife, it was impossible not to see the resemblance. Worse, something in her eyes betrayed a deep and painful understanding of what she interrupted. Charlie felt his heart sink down to his boots.

"Oh my God…" Lucille breathed softly, her hands covering her mouth.

Amy ignored her, but it looked like it took effort. She kept her eyes on Shilling still pressed to the window.

"Charlie, are you hurt?" she demanded.

"No…" he murmured, shaking his head.

"Let him go," she demanded of Argent. "He's mine."

"Yours?" Argent echoed, but his voice was strained and his sword already lowered. It looked like it would slip from his fingers any second.

"Come here, Charlie," Amy bid him.

He edged slowly around Argent. The Marquis all but ignored him. Once he reached Florin's side, he knew he was no longer her focus. She was watching the Argents. Her expression was pained and disappointed, but worse than that, it was mostly just resigned. Charlie stood as close to her as he dared, hovering in case there was anything he could do to fix this, but there wasn't. He knew that. That's why he'd been trying to avoid it. Of course, she was too clever for that. So he loitered by her shoulder, one hand slowly sneaking into the coat sleeve of the other arm, where his fingers desperately stimmed the button on his shirt cuff, trying to fidget subtly to relieve the tension.

"I'm not playing anymore," Florin declared to the room. "You two might treat this as some game of criminal recreation, but I was raised by the Lord Chief Justice of England — the only parent I've ever known. You are thieves and tricksters and murderers. Marquis Argent, I know you stole those diamonds and killed Monsieur Balles. Bonheur, you're lucky you're locked up with him instead of serving the time you're due."

Her accusations hung damningly in the air, like a storm of thunder and ice, waiting to crack.

"What would you do with us, Amelia?" Lucille whispered, breaking the silence.

Amy flinched. Charlie's hand tightened on his own wrist, squeezing to keep from clutching for her. Florin's expression was stricken as she looked at the woman on the bed, half-raised imploringly towards her. Shilling took a half step forward, placing himself deliberately in Lucille's line of sight. He stared her down. Argent might be the one with the sword, but he'd rather get stabbed in the back than leave Florin unguarded against Lucille's manipulations. Genuine or not.

"There is no fortune worth dying over," Charlie replied softly. "We solved the case. We know what happened. Everything else is window dressing."

"He's right," Amy agreed. "Neither of us need to get paid so badly we can't walk away."

"And you'll let us," Charlie turned his head to face

Argent, "because you know that we know that the police won't come after a Marquis in the name of his corrupt wife and a dead thief, no matter the depravity and injustice implicit."

"We can leave you to deal with each other however you see fit," Amy stated. Her tone was scathing to begin, but a slight tearful warble touched it at the end. She clenched her jaw a moment. "You certainly deserve each other."

The room hovered in the wake of their declarations. Both fell silent, but they didn't turn to go. Shilling wasn't sure if they were waiting to see if the Argents had anymore moves left, or if they just weren't quite ready to walk away. With Florin's reproachful judgement scalding Argent and Lucille, it felt unsafe to turn their backs.

Surprisingly, Jacques Argent was the first to move. He raised his sword, and Florin instantly moved hers to counter, but the action was unnecessary. He was only sheathing his blade. The Marquis' face had gone strangely hard and blank, as though he had begun to shut down when confronted with the truths before him. He turned his hands out to her placatingly, to show he meant no harm.

"Walk with me," he requested, moving towards the door.

They stood aside and he walked by, shutting the door to the tower and locking his wife back inside. Charlie considered commenting, and then decided not to start the fight again. The consequences were still unresolved from his first attempt, and Florin was likely to be the one to suffer for them. He'd never meant to do this to her.

They followed Argent back down the tower steps, moving slowly. No one said a word. The tension was so thick Charlie could feel his throat constricting. He was back to stimming his cuff button, trying to stave off the building pressure in his chest that felt like it might explode any minute.

When they reached the bottom of the stairs, Argent stopped. Amy stopped too. She was waiting for him. He had, after all, asked them to accompany him. Charlie swallowed nervously, trying to read the situation as best he could. There was nothing violent or threatening in Argent's demeanour. That was safe enough. Yet, he couldn't look at the two of them without reading the emotions they were attempting to hide. Their thinly veiled lies. There was so much pain there. It wasn't his, but he could feel it. He was choking on it. He squeezed the button on his cuff, rubbing it with his thumb and forefinger. The smooth round edge was soothing. It was the only soothing thing here. Not even Florin's perfume could take the edge off this conflict.

Argent looked on the brink of disembodiment. The agony in his eyes was absolute, yet there was a blankness over everything, an inability to process what was happening. His eyes refused to meet theirs and he couldn't stay still. He constantly turned this way and that, expressions chasing each other around his face like a chariot race. The anxiety was palpable. Charlie was sure that was where he was getting it from. Argent looked like he was contemplating his options and finding every single one a sheer cliff. He looked like a man about to jump.

Finally, he turned to face them. Without a word, he reached into a pocket in the lining of his jacket and drew out a small velvet drawstring bag. He held it out and when Florin raised her hand, pressed it into her palm.

"Take it," he insisted, his voice thick and distant. "Return them, keep them, do whatever you want with them. They're yours now."

Florin closed her hand over the bag slowly. She didn't check inside, and even Charlie didn't feel a need to verify the contents. They both knew what was in there. Argent looked away again as soon as he handed over the parcel of diamonds. He still looked like he was searching for something to hold his attention, while looking everywhere but at the woman before him.

"I have one request," he murmured to the floor.

Amy nodded slowly, not to agree, but to acknowledge she was prepared to hear him out. Despite keeping his eyes from her, he must have known, or taken her silence as permission.

"Stay," he whispered. "Just... just one night. Stay for a night and tell me your stories. Tell me... tell me of your adventures, how the two of you met, how you took down the Jack, tell me of your studies, of... of your life..."

The desperation and pain in Argent's voice made Charlie want to curl up in a ball and cry. He didn't understand how Florin was still standing, how she was so composed, but she was, and it was not his place to fall apart and embarrass her, even if he'd lost more air now than when he'd had a sword at his throat.

"We have the Jack's trial to return to in London," Amy replied softly.

Argent nodded, his acceptance agonised but understanding.

"But it's not until next week," she added. "If you'll have us, we could afford to stay three days."

Surprise lit up Argent's face and he turned suddenly to look at her, finally staring as though the shock of her offer outweighed his fear. She met his gaze patiently, and a timid and cautious hope began to dawn in both their eyes.

"*Oui*," he answered tenderly. "I would be delighted."

Charlie still wanted to curl up in a ball and pull a blanket over himself until he could breathe properly again. He couldn't imagine the feeling dissipating, and now he was going to have to navigate this stress for three days. Still, if it was what Florin wanted, then he would oblige as agreeably as he was physically able. It was the least he could do.

13

Breathing had become a fascinating event. Amy found that the breaths she took now were so slow and shallow her corset didn't even seem to strain. It stood to reason that she would eventually run out of air and faint, except that the technique she was using to suppress her emotions was also helping to meditate her body into a calm state. She would feel them eventually. She just had to filter them very slowly and carefully. If she had to feel everything she was feeling all at once in a single instant, she was certain she would explode.

Everything felt false, like it was all a dream and any minute she would wake, back at home, in her own bed, perhaps even Harry would be there and everything would be back to normal. Instead, she spent the afternoon in the garden with Argent. They had taken tea at a small table in the rose garden, and wandered the grounds after. Charlie had insisted they have their space, and then she had found him loitering in a tree. It was almost enough to make her wish normality away.

"Is he always like this?" Argent asked as they both stood and looked high into the upper branches where the sleuth seemed to be testing the boundaries of gravity and possibly even squirrel communication.

"I think so," she replied, unsure if she was apologising for his behaviour.

Charlie's pale coat had been carefully draped over one of the lower branches, where she could see the pockets of peculiar curiosities keeping it weighted down while he ventured into the upper reaches of madness. Even from this distance, she could see he had rolled the sleeves of his sky blue shirt to his elbows and his mousy hair looked golden in the sunlight. The nostalgia for her old life eased slightly, like a weight drifting from her chest.

"Really?" Argent asked softly. "Him?"

She thought about denying it, about playing dumb to force him to elaborate. After all, they had insisted on two rooms and, contrary to the papers Argent read, there was nothing romantic between them, but she couldn't stop staring at Charlie and there was no point trying to hide that.

"Your wife is a career criminal whom you have locked in a tower," she countered instead. "You don't get to judge."

Argent smiled at her. It was a winsome smile, amused and impressed, but also tinged with sadness. Everything he did was tinged with sadness now and it was hard to watch, thinking back on the man she had met that morning who had seemed so indestructibly confident. At least he might have the humanity now to feel guilty for what he'd done. Although, if she was honest, that wasn't what she wanted either.

"Do you wish for me to let her go?" he asked.

"I don't know what I wish," Amy sighed deeply.

"Besides, wishes are for djinn, fairies, and fools, and mine are all conflicting. By the right of law, the two of you should be thrown in prison for your crimes and left to share a cell. But I don't really want that either. I don't want people to suffer, but that's impossible, even for the people I care about, so what's the point in a wish?"

Argent's responding grimace was pained, like a parent who knew they could not wave a magic wand and fix the ills of their child. Worse still, like someone who wanted that to be their responsibility and wasn't sure they could be cast in the role.

"We are going to need to get him something," she continued, still watching Charlie move through the branches and starting to feel her heart palpitate at any sign that he might fall. A fall from that height would kill him, not that the notion had probably occurred to him.

"Something?" Argent asked.

"If we're going to be here for three days, we have to keep him occupied somehow — so he doesn't do anything stupid and hurt himself," she clarified. "A pottery studio, or some really strong cough medicine. The kind with opium in it."

Argent looked at her in alarm. Amy shrugged at him.

"He needs to keep busy," she said. "I've no idea what it is in his mind he has to keep so distracted from, but he goes a bit mad if he's not constantly occupied, or pacified with drugs. It's how his sisters manage him."

"I'm sure there's a spare room and some clay we can find..." Argent offered.

"*Merci,*" Amy smiled at him. "I might try and find

him some books too."

"I had no idea he was so…" Argent trailed off.

"Eccentric?" Amy smiled. "Charlie's a harmless kind of mad. At least he's never boring."

"I had heard he was eccentric," Argent smiled. "The stories that get published about him are quite… uh… outlandish. I take it from your rapport that the tales of your affair are untrue?"

Amy rolled her eyes and glared at the heavens. Argent smiled gently at her.

"Blatant, unfounded lies," she growled. "I swear there's a reporter who has it in for me. They've been stalking me since Harry was arrested."

"Have they…?" Argent commented dangerously.

"Whatever you're thinking of doing, don't," Amy ordered. "If I have to withstand another scandal, Charlie really will be the only person crazy enough to come near me."

"I get the impression you would not mind that so much…" Argent teased gently.

She gave him a dark side-eye, but his grin only widened.

"I'm fond of Charlie," she admitted, and left it at that.

"He must care for you as well," Argent replied. "Given his concern and behaviour here. I assume he was breaking Viviane out for you."

"It's hard to know," Amy admitted. "He has strange ways of showing affection, if he shows any at all. But I think that might just be the way he is. If medicine taught me anything, it's that when you get down to the bones of it, everyone is the same. People are simple creatures, and Charlie is no exception, even if has managed to cultivate an illusion of complexity about himself. He's extremely observant and emotionally intelligent. Unfortunately, he struggles to socialise because he can't always process the depth of his empathy. He can't show his feelings, because he's feeling too much. It just starts to manifest as nothing."

The two of them stood in the afterglow of her words, considering the strange man up the top of the tree, and just how relatable his condition could be in the right circumstance. Argent cleared his throat softly and whispered.

"Were you in love with him before the Jack of Hearts case, or was this a recent development?" he asked.

Amy bit her lip. She thought about arguing against his assertion, but there was no point.

"I didn't know him before that case," she admitted. Argent gave her a surprised look and she elaborated. "I mean, I knew of him, of course, we'd crossed paths, but I didn't *know* know him. Actually, our entire rapport just developed over that case, and I've barely seen him since… well, until this case… which he tried to warn me off. Except I think I have a better understanding of why he did that now…"

Argent was still staring at her in surprise. "You mean all this came about after knowing him for a single day?!"

"Well…" Amy shrugged half-heartedly. "One day can make a lot of difference. In the right situation, one day can completely change your life."

Argent's shoulders relaxed, dropping in appreciation of the sentiment. With one extremely tentative hand, he reached out and placed a supportive palm against her back. Amy leant back into his touch, letting the warmth of his fingers bleed through the back of her dress and soften her broken heart. Gently, almost imperceptibly, her shallow breaths deepened.

"*Oui...*" Argent agreed. "*Oui, absolument.*"

The night was dark and cool, but there was a chill in the air from something far more pervasive than the weather. Lucille was woken sharply when the door unlocked. Two of Argent's guards stormed the room. One unchained her from the bed while the other began to rifle through her drawers. The guard who unchained her dragged her down the stairs and she didn't dream of fighting back. If they were going to kill her, they already would have. If they were helping her on Amelia's orders, she didn't want to alert Jacques.

Amelia was not the one waiting for her in the entrance hall when they arrived. Few candles were lit and everything was ominously half-dark. Jacques stood in the half-light like a guardian and judge of the ninth circle of Hell. The guard hauled her to her husband and dumped her roughly in front of him, although she remained standing. Jacques stood, regal and cold, and stared at her with the blackest contempt. He said nothing.

Moments later, the second guard arrived and dumped a bag at Lucille's side, before holding out a coat for her to slide her arms into. She eyed the situation and turned to her husband.

"You're throwing me out?" she asked.

"I'm letting you go," he countered, like she should be grateful he'd consider even that.

"Where's Amelia? What happened?" she demanded.

"She's safe," Jacques replied. "She's upstairs in bed. We had dinner this evening and she told me about her ordeal with the Jack of Hearts — a terrifying situation you left her in."

"I didn't leave her in that!" Lucille snapped. "Henry Junior was still crawling when I left the Pound family. That is not on me."

"It is all on you!" Jacques roared at her.

She cowered from his accusation. It should have been loud enough to wake the house, but nothing else stirred. He'd never been this angry before. They'd had their ups and downs in the past, but Lucille had never seen him so homicidally furious. He looked like he could kill her. There was a pain in his eyes so deep and awful she would never have believed he could feel it if she hadn't seen it herself.

"You did this, Viviane," he condemned. "You did this. You stole my daughter — my *only child* — and you gave her to the English! You abandoned her! The culmination of events which had to transpire for her to even stumble onto my path..." he trailed off, shaking his head in grief. "I spent half my life believing you had stolen my heart... I never realised what that meant until now. I could have lived and died without ever knowing she existed! Now she is someone else's daughter! I never got the option! I never had the chance — the choice! You took that from me! From her! You took everything from us! I don't even know my own baby girl! Yes, Viviane, this is all on you. Everything that happened to her, everything you took from me." He motioned to the guard holding the coat, who shook it at her insistently. "I cannot change what you did, Viviane. There is nothing I can do, but I do not want to ever see you again. Never again. So, you have *deux* options. *Une,* leave here and never return. There is a carriage waiting outside that will take you to the village, and my doorstep will never welcome you again, not even in vengeance. *Deux,* defy me and stay, but risk having me change my mind and throw you back in that tower where I will eagerly forget you."

She stood in the aftershock of his ultimatum. Amelia was still here. She was just upstairs. If she heard them yelling she might come to investigate... might calm the situation...

But she also might just make it worse.

Lucille slipped her arms into the offered coat and pulled it tightly around herself, futilely attempting to ward off the chill. It was too deep for a mere coat to warm through.

"You don't leave me much choice..." she muttered.

"A lot more than you ever gave me," Argent damned her.

Lucille picked up her bag and walked away with it, but she stopped by the front door. Sure enough, there was a carriage waiting. Part of her wondered if the carriage was under strict instruction to drive her out past the village and then make absolutely sure that she never came back. That wasn't Jacques' style though. If he was going to kill someone, he usually did it himself. He wouldn't outsource her. If she was going to die by his order, then she would die by his hand. He was, for better or worse, a man of his word in that regard. He really was letting her go.

Still she stood, unmoving. Outside felt more welcoming than the hall behind her. The sight of the carriage brought a sweet taste of the freedom she had been yearning for. Her feet would not go forward. She turned to look over her shoulder. Jacques looked like the handsome villain of a romance novel, half shrouded in shadow. It was almost enough to make her believe she had loved him once, not just his money. It was a guilty reminder that the fool had loved her.

"I did what I thought was right," she told him. "We could not have raised her. Not into the woman she has become. We would have hated each other, and resented her for keeping us together. Believe it or not, I did do what was best for my daughter."

"Don't you dare tell me what kind of father I would have been," Jacques warned her menacingly. He took a step closer, looming over her like a phantom. "Get. Out."

His voice grated with ominous threat, as though he was a breath away from changing his mind. Lucille had nothing more to say and she wasn't going to risk any attempt to survive more of his vengeance than she already had. He'd caught her once, now she just needed to get far enough away that he'd never find her again, in case he did change his mind.

She didn't look behind her again. Not once she strode out to the carriage, nor when she climbed inside, nor once it began to roll away. She did not look back at the great estate she had once called home, and recently called prison. She did not look back for any glimpse of the man she had called husband. She didn't even look back to see if perhaps there was a small face watching from a window, one last glimpse of someone she had barely met, yet somehow still knew. That, at least, caused her a slight pang. An unusual stab of grief that she had only felt once before.

The worst thing about the wealthy, in Charlie's opinion, was that they employed staff to run their lives. If he was completely honest, the worst thing was actually the inherent hoarding of wealth, partnered with upholding an oppressive class system, and casually privileged bigotry. But this morning he had been lounging in bed, with no desire to ever move again, face half buried in pillows, when some well-meaning French maid had come to check on him to make sure he was getting up and readying himself for breakfast, or at least not feeling poorly, which meant get out of bed.

Disgraceful. He had earnt this rest.

But he was not allowed to indulge it. In truth, the

only reason he was allowed to indulge it at home was because his sisters thought it was good for him to stay out of everyone else's way, and they had trained their staff to avoid him — except Jasper. The first time he had vocalised these beliefs, Rebecca had pointed out that the ability to lounge around in bed all day made him one of the wealthy. The Pence siblings across the road did not have such luxury. He had decided it was best not to raise it with her after that.

When he came down to breakfast, Florin and Argent were already eating and he had half a mind to run off, but she caught his eye and beckoned him over. He was pleased for her sake that the two of them were getting along so well, but he didn't want to intrude. Except that there was bread. French bread. Charlie would never speak of this to Michael so long as he lived, but the French really knew their bread, and he was far too weak a man to resist it.

As he joined them, mostly just for the bread but also a spot of tea, he noticed a folded newspaper sitting on the table near Argent. He cocked his head to the side as he regarded it, scanning the available inches to deduce the paper. It was written in English and part of the title was visible. The Daily Telegraph, he concluded. The front page was dominated by a story about a stolen painting. When he looked away from it, Amy was smiling at him.

"Curious?" she inquired.

"Sated," he replied.

"You're not itching to get back to England to find out who stole it?" she teased.

"I know who stole it," he sighed, munching on a perfect crust of baguette.

The look she gave him was utterly disparaging and Argent began to laugh softly. Charlie looked between them in confusion.

"You've glimpsed half an article on a folded newspaper — which we both know is regularly full of tripe — and you already know what happened?" she huffed. "Why? Did Bonheur do this one as well?"

"I wouldn't put it past her, but no," he replied. "There's something of a collector's war going on between several members of the British aristocracy. I've tried my best to keep out of it, given my dislike of them, their methods, and their general taste in art." He munched his bread contemplatively. "However, if someone steals a Delacroix, I will be more interested."

Argent seemed to approve. Although, possibly, it was just his usual smug self-satisfaction.

"Wouldn't put it past her?" Amy echoed. "You really think Bonheur could steal a painting from inside that tower?"

"She organised stealing those diamonds from inside that tower," Charlie reminded. "Besides, she's not there anymore — not that I think she's had time to get to Britain for some light B&E."

"Oh Charlie..." Amy gave him a look. "You didn't..."

"Not me." He shook his head, taking a fresh slab of bread and pouring a cup of tea.

Florin looked to Argent, and he considered her with solemn patience.

"I let her go," he admitted. "*Monsieur* Shilling was correct, it was pointless to keep her here. I found no contentment striving for vengeance, and keeping her under my roof was only serving to remind me how unattainable it was. I offered her a carriage to the station last night, but warned her that she is not permitted to return or her life will be in danger. I never want to see that woman again."

"She left then?" Florin asked softly. "Just like that?"

"Just like that," Argent agreed. A small pause hovered at the table, like a bubble of hope that they recognised was Amy's optimism that Lucille might have left a message or a note. Argent clearly didn't want to pop it, but her anticipation died without his help. He did add, with a trace of melancholy, "I was not kind in my dismissal. There was not much time for her to consider her options, however she chose to measure them."

Charlie cocked his head as he considered that. For all Argent's faults, and Charlie felt there were many, he appreciated that the man recognised his own behaviour. He didn't apologise for it or seek to rectify it, but he acknowledged it, and that did a little to compensate him in Charlie's eyes. The Marquis wasn't fooling himself that he was a tragic hero in this tale. He knew in the story of himself and his wife, there were only villains.

"She made her choice," Florin agreed. "And she wasn't kind in her thievery either."

Charlie grimaced at the tightness in her voice. That was exactly the kind of pain he'd been hoping to spare her by keeping her away from the Argents, not that he had remotely succeeded in any regard. He huddled in his chair, with his bread and tea, and tried not to make anything worse. A small voice in the back of his head that sounded suspiciously like Rebecca reminded him that this wasn't about him and he was not responsible for Florin or her family.

Somehow, that was about as helpful as shoes without soles. The guilt did not shift. Undoubtedly, there was another story somewhere in that folded up newspaper about Harry Pound and his upcoming trial that they were due to return for soon. The guilt solidified like unchewed bread in his stomach.

"No," Argent agreed, and a sly smile touched the corners of his lips as his fingertips tapped the newspaper. "It sounds like she uncovered quite a scandal stealing those diamonds though."

"Oh, that was just Charlie," Amy dismissed, to Shilling's displeasure. "He stumbled into that all on his own."

"Because of the diamonds..." Charlie muttered into his teacup.

"I'm surprised the Telegraph is bothering with the gossip, although I suppose they have to announce that the wedding they initially reported never happened," Amy sighed.

"It's only mentioned in relation to an interview with a Lady Sterling, who claims to have hired the two of you to work a case," Argent smiled.

"Why is that in the paper?" Charlie grumbled. He knew Lionel Tanner loved to stalk his cases (some more effectively than others), but this wasn't high-profile enough, surely. Unless Sterling was announcing what had been stolen.

"It's in response to yesterday's article misrepresenting that the two of you eloped to France," Argent smiled.

Charlie choked on his tea. He would have loved to claim it was a delicate splutter, but he breathed far too much hot liquid and hid behind his hands as he coughed and wheezed. He could feel Florin and Argent looking at each other, and refused to re-join the conversation until it no longer involved him.

"They said we what?" Florin demanded.

"This is the same paper that suggested the two of you were having an affair when you caught the Jack," Argent reminded. "It is hardly a surprise. Although, it is disappointing to note that most of the tales about you are probably false."

"About the two of us, certainly," Amy huffed, blushing deeply. "Lots of the ones about Charlie are still true."

"Oh, are they?" Charlie coughed behind his hands.

"Well, plenty of them must be true enough," Amy insisted. "I remember when you caught that slave trafficker, and then the time those pirates tried to rob the Queen—"

Charlie groaned loudly at the memories. When people described his work out loud, his life sounded a lot more colourful than it actually was. It made the ridiculous sound plausible. It made Tanner imbecilically declaring their elopement less far-fetched.

Besides, as far as Florin was concerned, the only reason she actually knew there were any shreds of truth to those stories was because in both cases Charlie had been forced to work with Lord Pound, whom his partner was very obviously going out of her way not to mention at the moment. He hadn't heard the words 'father' or 'daddy' pass her lips since she'd saved Charlie from Argent in the tower.

The observation was a sharp reminder that he was not in a position to begrudge her anything. He'd known exactly who he'd been chasing when he'd told Florin she could come along, which meant a good, sharp slab of this was his fault.

The problem currently was that he couldn't meet her eye. She had become flustered at the announcement from the paper. He had heard the embarrassment in her voice. But she had also shrugged it off much faster than he had. She was an expert at dismissing nonsense. He always had been. It was harder now than it used to be. It was harder with her.

Lucille had accused him of being in love with her daughter.

He rather thought the woman was full of gossip and spite.

It did not do to dwell on such things.

So why had he choked at the notion of eloping with her?

And why didn't it seem like such a terrible idea? Why, suddenly, were all the memories of her perfume on his pillow, and their kiss at her graduation party, and every allusion anyone had ever made about them, including the one Argent had made about them sharing a bed, compounding in his head? And why, somehow, were they not really so sudden after all?

If Lucille was right after all, he should be elated.

Instead, he was terrified.

Florin was easily the most remarkable person he'd ever met. The confidence with which he felt that only further served to prove Lucille right. Which in turn deepened his fear.

"Charlie?" Amy addressed him in concern. "Are you all right?"

"May I be excused?" he muttered to his plate.

"Of course," she answered, without bothering to check with their host. Charlie didn't wait for his approval.

"If you need me, I will be in the conservatory," he announced, eyes resolutely downcast. Florin had organised for the conservatory to be repurposed as a pottery studio for him during their stay. It was one of the many things that made her wonderful. That thought should not have felt like a hot knife in the back, but it did. This required consideration. The kind of deep, mulling consideration that needed to keep his hands busy. Twisting his ring and stimming his buttons would not be enough. He needed to throw clay.

14

The days passed in a blur. They felt like they were over before they began, and Amy was sad to see them go, especially when she knew she was returning to Harry's trial and London gossip and the bleak looming outcomes of both. She was looking forward to seeing her father again, although she wouldn't say that out loud. She hadn't really spoken much about her family to Argent, and she hadn't called him by anything but name. They hadn't discussed it in words. They weren't there yet.

However, it was her dearest hope that, in time, with Henry included as well, they would be.

Still, days spent on the idyllic French estate, getting to know the complicated man that was Jacques Argent, and spending time with Charlie, were some of the best ways she had ever spent her time. Charlie, unfortunately, was going madder by the minute. However, when the rest of reality felt so far away, it was easier to be patient with him. That was all he seemed to need, and she felt like she understood. His brain was painfully loud, all the time, and he needed people to be soft with him.

Argent never seemed to pass up the opportunity to

rib her about her capacity to be gentle with the socially dysfunctional sleuth. She was forced to resist the urge to slap them both. The notion that the extent of her affection might be so transparent was concerning, but there was nothing to be done about it. Apparently, she wasn't alone.

The time had come and her bags were packed. She stood on the front drive with Argent as the carriage was loaded up and the two of them embraced tightly and kissed each other's cheeks. She was sorry to be leaving and she said as much.

"I am more sorry to see you go," he insisted. "It has been truly wonderful getting to know you, Amelia. I will never be the same. Although, I will be less sad to see the last of your partner. I am concerned how many staff I might be losing to him."

"He promised not to start another revolution," Amy assured. Privately, she was less convinced, having walked in on him the other day bellowing to the staff about how if Napolean hadn't restored the monarchy and seized the crown, France could have become a beacon of democracy.

Argent shook his head in disbelief. "You've been here three days and already I have five servants who think they love him. I must admit... I am at a complete loss as to the appeal."

"Charlie has a knack for inadvertently appealing to the working class," she confessed. "He says things that he thinks are purely logical — from an anarchic standpoint — but come across as flattery. Everyone likes to hear that someone else thinks they deserve the world, even if they're being told to rise up and claim it for themselves. It probably helps that he's spent most of that time half naked and sculpting in your conservatory."

"That pale stick?" Argent raised an eyebrow.

"You'd be surprised how much it helps," she admitted.

Argent gave her that teasing look again. She didn't shy away from it this time. After all, he'd just admitted that five of his staff also saw the appeal. No one expected Charlie to look good with his shirt off, covered in clay, and generally unkempt, but he did.

"Will he at least settle his behaviour while you travel?" Argent asked. "You are supposed to be his partner, not his keeper."

"He's not good without work," Amy sighed. "But I think we've found a happy medium. I gave him a project for the trip home at least."

"*Bien*," Argent conceded. He took her hands in his. "And you will write?"

"*Oui*, of course," Amy promised. "I will write and I'll come back to visit again. If it weren't for the trial, I'd be tempted to stay longer. And you! You must write and come and see us whenever you're in London."

"*Oui*, of course," he echoed her softly, kissing her cheek again.

Amy caught a glimpse of pale coat in the doorway, but it vanished, and she smiled to herself. He was the strangest man she'd ever met, but he was kind — in his own way. He tried so hard to be.

"Charlie!" she called into the house. "Are you ready

yet?"

He gave an appropriate pause to disguise his loitering before stumbling out of the house, lugging his own case insistently.

"Sorry about the hold up, Florin," he apologised, staring resolutely at the driveway as he crossed to the carriage and loaded his own bag. The footmen were indeed watching him with the soft admiration Amy always felt in herself when she watched him, and seemed rather disappointed but unsurprised that he refused their help. She was too amused by his false apology to dismiss it, and the fact that he was oblivious to everyone else's fondness for him. When he turned back to her, his head tilted curiously, that way he did that, unbeknownst to him, made her start to melt.

"Ready when you are," she told him.

He nodded, and she could see him fidgeting with his ring. He wanted to be gone, and he didn't want to have to socialise to do it. She managed to walk him through an appropriate goodbye to their host, before giving Argent one last squeezing embrace and jumping in the carriage. If she didn't go then, she never would.

The last few days had been a delightful dalliance with a life she could have had. There was a part of her that had privately wondered if she could have stayed forever and forgotten all her troubles. But life wasn't that easy. It wasn't that simple. She couldn't just leave her father. In truth... she couldn't just leave Harry. As much as she had been trying to ignore him, that part of her life wasn't over. It didn't feel over. Hiding from it brought her no closure.

The thought of it settled like unpleasant London smog in the carriage as it drove away from Argent's estate, and she didn't look back for fear she would change her mind and stay. Instead, she reached out and took Charlie's hand. She linked her fingers in his and rested her head against his hair. He startled at the affection, but didn't draw away.

"Oh, shut up," she dismissed his uncertainty. She knew he didn't feel the same, that he just wasn't that kind of person, and that was fine. She wasn't asking him to. But he was her friend, he had gotten her into this mess, and she just needed someone to support her a little while she walked away from everything she could have been. Even then, there wasn't a single regret. For all Charlie's hesitations regarding her involvement, this had been the adventure of a lifetime.

The boat back to England was a gentle trip and an intense relief. Shilling didn't realise he'd missed home so much. It had never even occurred to him, with everything else going on, that he might be homesick. He'd just assumed the nausea was his unresolved feelings for Florin, which he'd decided were best left unresolved, before torturing himself further by reading her manuscript. There was something agonising about reading erotic fiction written by the woman he was infatuated with.

It occurred to him then that perhaps he had been

killed by the Jack of Hearts and now he was just living through whichever circle of Hell was reserved for people like him. However, that was clearly the emotions talking rather than logic, and he was loath to give Dante's speculations even the slightest credit. Charlie had no proof of an afterlife. It was a philosophical conundrum for those struggling with a crisis of existence, of which he was now one.

He sat on the boat and tapped his pencil on the pages before him. She had beautiful handwriting. Absentmindedly, he prodded the end of the pencil against his face a few times. It didn't make him feel more alive. Florin had clearly spent the months since Harry's arrest keeping herself occupied. Her work was inspired, and a long way from their reality. She had also been doing research, but he already knew that.

A strangely depressing yet freeing thought occurred to him. Florin had not been interested in Harry, as Charlie had deduced before they had discovered he was he was a serial killer. He had assumed it was because Amy saw him as a brother, after being raised in the same house, by the same people, with the same father. Logically, that made perfect sense to him. It was a strange arrangement, not that the aristocracy did anything that wasn't strange. Except, now he recalled her choice in lover once her fiancé had been removed from the picture. There was a very good chance Florin wasn't attracted to men, not that he'd really thought she'd be interested in him personally anyway.

The knife in his chest eased, and he decided to make the most of the revelation. He'd never felt this way about anyone before. At first, he had simply lumped her in with his friends, knowing that he cared for her with the same tenderness he cared for Michael or Julian, but it wasn't quite the same. There was a tightness in his chest and a fog in his brain no one else brought out in him. Yet, it helped to think that she was more inclined the way of his sisters, and perhaps he could treat her as such. Everything else would follow in time.

He packed up the manuscript carefully, buttoning it back into its folder. Then he stood and went looking for Florin. She was outside, watching the waves in the late evening sun. Backlit by the sunset, a few loose curls wafting in the breeze, she did cause his chest to ache horribly. That kind of nonsense wouldn't do. He huffed away his feelings with a deep sigh, and headed towards her.

She smiled at him when she saw him approaching, and he nearly decided to simply keel over from a heart attack right then and there, but that felt overly dramatic. Instead, he sidled up to her, eyes downcast, and handed over the folder before nervously beginning to rub a button on the front of his coat and watch the ocean.

"Hello Charlie," she smiled, taking the folder back.

His throat felt strangely stuck. He took a deep slow breath and spoke gently.

"It's a very excellent book, Florin," he told her, stimming his button. "Very Alice Jones. You should be extremely pleased with it."

"Alice Jones?" she echoed. "You think so?"

"Absolutely," he smiled. "You completely captured that flavour, I think. There were a few instances where the language was more yours than hers, but you did an excellent job of emulating her. I'm half tempted to let her know about it next time I write to her. I think she'd be honoured."

"Well, I'm not sure what I'm going to do with it," she admitted, blushing softly from the praise. "At the moment it's for our eyes only, I suppose…"

Something about the way she said that renewed the deep inferno Charlie was presently trying to smother. Against his better judgement, he looked up. Now it was her turn not to meet his eyes. She hugged the folder to her chest and stared into the distant sunset across the waves. Charlie had never seen anything so beautiful in his life. Just like that, the fire went out.

He did love Amelia Florin.

And that was just fine. His life was richer for having that experience, and he had no need for her to love him back. They were friends. Companions. Partners. She was in his life and that was enough.

"Well, if you change your mind, you should contact Dawson & Kropp," he encouraged. "See if you can ghost write for them."

"Oh, I don't think it's that good," she shook her head.

"I've read everything they've published. It's better than some of them," he insisted. "I certainly devoured it."

"Yes, well, you're clearly trying to distract yourself from a perilous moral dilemma," she sighed, leaning on the railing with her arms around her manuscript.

Charlie stared at her, panic renewed. The woman

was good, but how in God's name was she that good?! How could she possibly know how he felt?

"I don't blame you…" she continued. "And I know things feel more complicated than they actually are…"

Charlie couldn't even think of a defence. He stood completely frozen. The heart attack might not be optional anymore. He couldn't breathe. Her words were going in, but he wasn't sure he was processing them.

"But it is a strange situation," she continued. "For me, personally. I… I guess… I guess I mean thank you. Thank you for not contacting the police."

Oh. That. Reality crashed back over him like a cold bucket of water. He made a mental note never to try and make things about himself ever again. Of course she had more going on than his undisclosed feelings for her. In truth, it was a conundrum he had been avoiding at the estate. The ultimate quandary. Ignoring justice for the sake of personal concern. Still, he had found a way to justify his weak stance, even if the truth of it was so depressing that drowning in lovelorn self-pity was preferable.

"You're welcome, Florin," he sighed, leaning on the railing and looking out at the horizon with her. "You're right about the moral dilemma. However, ultimately, I think we can accept that this one is out of our hands. We solved our case. We can return to Sterling successful — should you choose to."

"Should I choose to?" she laughed, turning to face him.

He grinned wryly, appreciating her incredulity.

"You think I'm the type to take after my mother?" she pressed.

"You have her cunning and her wit, but no," he smiled softly at the sunset, "and I'm sure even those attributes you have made your own. I mean only that the prize is yours, and you are free to do as you see fit."

"Hm," Florin mused to the railing. She reached into her bodice and Charlie stared fixatedly at the edge of the coast he could see in the distance. He kept his eyes there so resolutely he almost missed the pouch she was handing him. She took his hand forcefully, demanding his attention, and depositing the small velvet bag in his palm. It was as soft and warm as a baby bunny, and he could barely bring himself to grasp it. "It's your case, Charlie. You finish it. Thank you for letting me tag along."

"It's impossible to finish, Florin," he countered. "Even if I return the diamonds…" he trailed off.

"I know," she sighed. "And I'm sorry."

"It's not you," Charlie insisted. "It's not you, Florin. I know I should report what we learnt about Balles' murderer, but I also know the court will never do anything. A known thief who would have hanged anyway was killed by an esteemed Marquis — no one will care. Argent was right about that. Balles would have swung. No one will ever care that he was murdered, and that is wrong, but I don't know what to do about it. The system is corrupt, corrupt and broken, and I… I can't… I can't change that. I've never been able to change it."

"That's never stopped you before," Florin reminded

him carefully. "You've never shied away from protesting the system, Charlie. Not until now. You really want to tell me that's the problem? You want me to believe you didn't tell the police about Jacques Argent because you didn't think it would do any good, not because he's my father?"

Charlie pursed his lips and frowned petulantly at the sky, pocketing the diamonds and trying to find his way out of this one. He looked out over the railing again, scrunching his hair in his fingers and contemplating her accusation. It was undoubtedly true, but it wasn't the whole truth. It was a small truth inside a larger truth, as all things were.

"You knew, didn't you?" she pressed him. "Before we started any of this, you knew who my birth parents were — both of them. A secret previously known only by my mother. You knew Lucille Bonheur was one of her aliases, you knew exactly who we were chasing, and you knew Argent was my father before we pursued the case there. You knew all of that and you never said anything."

"I... tried to warn you..." he muttered defensively to the horizon. "I was trying to protect you from... from the truth..." It sounded terrible when he said it out loud.

"Charlie," she addressed him tartly.

He turned to face her and she slapped him across the cheek. It wasn't hard, but it was pointed. She'd slapped him worse before, for things he had deserved much less. This one he was prepared to accept.

"Don't ever keep things like that from me again," she

ordered. "Not ever. It was my business, Charlie. I deserved to know."

"Agreed," he sighed, rubbing his cheek. "I'm sorry, Florin. I was in the wrong. I know that now. I just… I just didn't want you to get hurt again. The last time you helped me with a case it destroyed your life. This one had the potential to do the same. I… I couldn't bear to see you get hurt. Not like that. Not again. Not by them."

Before he knew what was happening, she grabbed him. One arm pulled him in tightly, while the other kept the manuscript folder pressed between them, and she planted her lips to his cheek exactly where she had just struck him.

"I know why you did it, Charlie," she breathed against his skin. "The method to your madness was very sweet, as always. Just promise me you'll never do it again."

"Okay," he agreed stupidly as she let him go. "I'm sorry. I'll tell you next time."

She laughed and he cursed himself silently. Like there was going be a next time they discovered her secret birth parents. Stupid. He could feel the heat in his cheeks, and he quickly smoothed his coat, tracing his finger around the rim of one of the buttons, letting the repetitive action sooth him. She shouldn't be allowed to just grab him and kiss him like that. There should be rules against it. Now she was looking at him like she was worried there was something wrong with him, like he couldn't breathe properly. In fairness, that was presently dubious.

"You're very confusing, Florin," he muttered

breathlessly. "Slapping people and then kissing them. It's confounding."

"Well, I'm conflicted," she replied. "I'm angry that you hid so much from me, but I'm grateful that you care and that you brought me in on the case, even though I understand now why you really didn't want to."

"Hm," Charlie conceded reluctantly. "I understand that."

"Of course you do," she smiled, a soft blush darkening her own cheeks as she turned from him to lean on the railing again, extending them both some space. "You're really very clever, most of the time. When you're not trying to hide things from me."

Guilt and humble gratitude chased each other around his stomach. If he was going to do better, this was the best time to start, and he had seen something she ought to know about.

"She was at the ferry terminal," he blurted, unsure if he was doing the right thing and wondering how that had become a matter of such confusion. "Bonheur, Elizabeth Florin, she was at the ferry terminal this afternoon. I saw her. She saw us. I don't know if you saw her, but she didn't try and approach, so I let it be, but I didn't say anything because... well, because I didn't want to bring it up if the two of you didn't want to bring it up..."

"She was there?" Florin echoed, looking back at him.

Charlie nodded apologetically.

"Huh," Florin hummed, turning back again and looking to the water.

Charlie stood and watched and waited. She didn't

say anything else. He continued to wait, but she all but ignored him. He wasn't sure if he was in trouble again. It didn't feel like he was in trouble, but he wasn't always sure. It could be hard to tell. He approached cautiously and leant on the railing with her, their elbows touching.

"Is that her real name?" Florin asked quietly.

Charlie looked to her, cocking his head curiously for clarification. A deep grin split Florin's face as she looked at him, and she turned her expression bashfully away almost instantly.

"Is Elizabeth Florin her real name?" she asked the railing.

"Unlikely," he replied. "But in truth I have no idea. The earliest name I ever found for her was Bonny O'Hare, but I'm not sure that's real either."

"Why were you even looking?" she asked.

"I was curious," he shrugged. "I had just started working for Henry, immediately after the human trafficking case, so I was used to trying to trace people anyway. I wanted to know more about him. You were the most interesting thing I could uncover. I wanted to know more and I thought, perhaps, if he ever wanted to know more, it wouldn't hurt to have the information ready and waiting for him."

"You've known all these years and you never said anything?!" she exclaimed, turning to face him.

Now Charlie knew he was in trouble again, but, honestly, it was getting too difficult to keep track of. He shrugged helplessly at her, wondering what he was going to have to apologise for next.

"No one ever asked," he replied in kind.

She stared at him and he blinked defencelessly back at her. Slowly, softly, she began to laugh, and gently buried her face in the shoulder of his coat. He stood there, dumbfounded, leaning on the railing and wondering how on Earth humanity had ever learnt to communicate in the first place — if indeed it could be claimed they had.

They stayed like that for a while. Charlie decided that he couldn't be in too much trouble if Florin was laughing and happy enough to lean against him. Eventually, she shifted position and settled for nuzzling in against him, resting her head on his hair, and linking her arm in his elbow. It was, altogether, quite lovely.

"Charlie...?" she murmured.

"Yes, Florin?" he replied.

"I know all these disasters bother you," she sighed. "That nasty business with the Jack of Hearts, and this whole ordeal with Sterling's diamonds, and all the things about them that affect me, and I'm moved that you care so much — that it concerns you so deeply — but I want you to know I don't regret any of it. Without all those unpleasantries, Charlie, I never would have befriended you. You really are wonderful, in your own strange way, and I don't say that enough. You care like no one else I've ever met. You care about everyone, so deeply, even if you manifest it as a call to revolution. Watching you tear yourself apart the last few days, trying to decide between justice and compassion... it awes me." There was a pause and she gave a small, sentimental laugh. "I'm sorry, I don't mean to unsettle you. I just wanted you to know how deeply I admire your kind heart, how much I've come to love it, and that given the choice, I truly wouldn't be without you."

Charlie stayed absolutely silent and held himself like a statue. She didn't seem to need a response, but he didn't feel he could leave that statement unresolved.

"Nor I you," he replied affectionately.

Her hand tightened warmly on his sleeve as she hugged his arm. This. This was exactly what he had been hoping for. This was enough. Maybe he did care for her with a slightly different intensity than his other friends, but treating her just the same, having her treat him the same, knowing that they had each other's best interests at heart, that was good enough. Knowing she was happy, right now, in this moment, standing with him at the railing of the ship, that was just perfect.

They had the briefest of stops that night in a small inn before the earliest train in the morning. The last minute trip back to London to ensure the longest possible stay with Argent certainly had its consequences. Amy was beginning to feel them. She was tired, and not just from the travel. There was an emotional exhaustion from the last few months she wasn't sure she would ever shift. The night was colder too, colder than she expected, certainly. There was a chill in the air she couldn't quite explain, like a ghost stepping over her grave.

She didn't want to spend the night alone.

But she didn't have a choice. Charlie had been

endlessly patient with her recently, and she still felt bad about making him freeze up on the boat. His affection was earnest, but platonic. That was just the way he was and she needed to stop confusing him. Her little school girl crush wasn't his fault.

At least, that was what she kept telling herself.

In the cold, dark room of the inn, she couldn't help but wonder if Argent was right, if this was more than just a little crush. It certainly felt like love. They had spoken of it several times. She understood his concern. Every father worried about their daughter's choice in suitor. He had always seemed so surprised, not just that she was fond of so strange a man, but that she hadn't done anything about it.

The half of her that she had decided was the recently discovered French half wanted to change that. She wanted to storm into the next room and curl up in Charlie's bed with him, even if he wasn't the type to take things any further. But that wasn't fair on him, and the truth of that twisted in her stomach, making her feel guilty for all the little things she had thought and spoken to try and justify her desire. She could almost feel Argent's knowing eyes still watching her.

The look he had given her when she had told him about the kiss in Henry's office was seared onto her soul. She had finally been forced to admit the truth out loud. The whole truth. He had kissed her, yes, but in order to provoke Harry. It had worked like a charm.

However, for someone who only kissed her to smear lipstick on his mouth, it had certainly felt like he'd meant it.

That was the whole truth. The other half that she'd been hiding. The half that knew no one else had ever kissed her like Charlie had. Not before, not since.

Argent had advised her to tell Charlie that, but it seemed like cruel advice. Firstly, the words weren't easy to summon. The very thought of it constricted her throat like a choking hand of death. Secondly, what was Charlie supposed to do with that knowledge once she lumped it on him? He'd never shown romantic interest in anyone before. Even Bronny had washed her hands of inspiring sexual interest from him. Everyone who knew Charlie knew he was passionate about puzzles, not people. He'd never looked twice at another human before, unless he thought they'd committed a crime. It wasn't fair.

But that was life.

It wasn't fair she felt this way about him. It wasn't fair he didn't feel the same. But unrequited love was an ordinary part of life. Most people had to live through it. She could be one of them.

Just when she had talked herself into ignoring all Argent's advice, she found a note slipped inside the opening of her bag. It wasn't a long letter, but the thick cream envelope that contained it gave it a comfortable weight.

It also wasn't what she thought.

Her eyes fell on the elegant handwriting and continued helplessly across the message, unable to look away despite herself.

My Dearest Amelia,
If you read this instead of burning it, I applaud your

generosity. I would never begrudge you the latter. Of course, now that there's a chance I have your attention, I honestly don't know what I could ever say.

I'm sorry.

It seems like the most appropriate place to start, but the words feel meaningless simply putting ink to paper. I could never truly convey what I mean by them. There is no way to communicate all the things I have felt across all these years. I wanted to do right by you, but I don't think I ever knew what that meant.

I wanted you to have the best of things, as I never did. I wanted you to grow up loved and wealthy and cared for, with every conceivable opportunity, never wanting for anything. Your young man gave cutting voice to my many demons the other day by pointing out the sharp truth I have always tried to hide from myself — that by my choice you would only want for a mother. As someone who never wanted for my own, I didn't think that would be so great a loss for you. Surely losing me would improve your life. But I can see too how unfair it was to take that choice from you, even if I thought it was best.

You have grown into someone the likes of which I can hardly imagine. Whether or not you hate me for all I've done, I am comforted to see the confidence and brilliance that has blossomed in you. I could never in a million years have imagined a child of mine would be smart enough to be a doctor, and it helps me think that perhaps I did a little bit right by you, even if it was against the odds.

I am very glad to see you have much better taste in men than I do. He might not be as handsome or as prosperous as I would have wished for you, but that boy is clever and he loves you. I could only wish for someone in all my years who would have defended me with half the fire he is prepared to fight for you. I know he'll take care of you, and if by some inconceivable miracle he doesn't, he knows that I am just as good at finding people as he is. He has been warned.

I don't know if you would ever want to have anything to do with me, and if you didn't I would understand. I can also appreciate the wisdom of keeping your distance from a notorious criminal that both your fathers would no doubt clap in chains, or worse. I will not pretend that I would ever have been a good mother, or that I would even know where to start now.

However, if you ever need me, for anything, let it be known. Put the word out. I will find you. If nothing else, tell your boy. He will always know how to find me if you need me.

You don't have to believe me, and I don't even know if you're still reading this far, but I do love you, Amelia. In a way unlike anything I have known in this world. Thank you for becoming the wonderful woman you are. It's enough to inspire hope in the stone heart of a deeply flawed woman. A reluctant but blessed mother.

With all the love, my darling, that I have ever known,
Mum

Amy didn't know when she'd started to cry, but when she lay her head on her pillow, with the letter still scrunched in her hand, she buried her face in the fabric and wept endlessly and bitterly until she finally lost consciousness.

15

The morning was a pained, exhausted blur. When she described it that way to Charlie while they were on the train, he replied that that's what most mornings were. His glib but earnest assessment of life was almost enough to take the edge off. He had woken her when it was still dark, while she had been deep in the clutch of sleep with the crumpled letter and tear-stained pillow. That meant he knew. She'd had no opportunity to try and hide it from him. She wondered if that meant he knew what the letter said about him. He didn't strike her as the type to read her private correspondence, but it was Charlie Shilling. He had ways of knowing. If he did know, he didn't say anything.

He did hang attentively close as they travelled, which she appreciated. Whether through affection or concern, she was too tired to care. The exhaustion of the trip, the emotional exhaustion of it, had been compounded by her mother's letter. It was like being dropped in thick mud and beaten five feet deep with a sledgehammer. The important thing was that she had Charlie, and they were nearly home. Then they would just have to survive another hellish week faced with the Jack of Hearts trial.

That, more than anything, began to drive home the extent to which choices weren't hers. Her mother's letter had talked of denying her choices, of making questionable ones. It didn't matter if Amy wanted to throw caution to the wind and declare her love for Charlie. She couldn't. Not with Harry's trial. The choice wasn't hers. The newspapers were bad enough, but she and Charlie were almost certainly going to have to sit through hours of questioning while Harry's lawyers tried to make them look guilty of fabrication and collaboration. If anyone found her in Charlie's bed, they'd almost have a case.

Everything about the situation was depressing, but she focused on the good things. She was back with plenty of time to help Laura and Jane plan their wedding. She was going to see her father again. They had called and left a message to let him know which train they'd be on, and she was hoping he would meet them at the station. She hadn't said anything else. Everything else about their adventure she wanted to tell him in person. Especially what they'd found.

Charlie collected their bags when the train pulled in and they came down the stairs to the station. He was even scruffier than usual this morning, and Amy had to constantly resist the urge to straighten his hair. It looked like birds had been nesting in it. She wanted to run her fingers through it and pat it down and trace the lines of his crooked face, down his broken nose and slanted lips. She wanted to live her parents' perception of them. He gave her a quizzical look when he saw her watching, tipping his head to the side like he always did. The gesture made her melt, and she closed her eyes and turned away even as she smiled, so that she didn't have to look at what she knew she was walking away from.

When they came into the main station, Henry was waiting for them near the platform café. He came towards them hesitantly and Amy dashed over at the sight of him. She flew towards him and embraced him tightly, burying her face in the lapel of his coat.

"It's so good to see you, Daddy!" she exclaimed, worried she might start crying again after everything else.

He squeezed her back, but otherwise stayed stoically silent. She could feel him looking over her shoulder, giving Charlie a nod. His woollen coat was scratchy against her face, but he was warm, and he smelled like home, and she had an almost overwhelming feeling that everything was about to be all right. Until she saw his expression.

The change started quickly. It took her a moment to let him go and step back, but once she did, she could see his face was ashen and deeply lined with emotion. There was a quiver to the set of his lips that spoke to the real reason he hadn't greeted either of them with words yet. Charlie had noticed it first, because of course he had. As soon as she looked back over her shoulder at him, she could see the concern painted thick across his face. His sharp grey eyes flickered across their surroundings and he snatched a folded newspaper from a nearby table, cursing violently.

"Charlie!" she exclaimed, surprised at the language.

Henry's hands still clasped hers, and his grip

tightened momentarily. She turned back to him, trying to work out what was going on. She was so tired, and everything suddenly felt so wrong. Her dad stood before her, his face sagged with pain and his thumbs stroking the backs of her hands weakly as he clutched them.

"Amy, darling," he began thickly, his voice coming deep and slow and soft, "Harry's dead."

It was the first time he'd said Harry's name since that fateful night. The words echoed. It was so strange. The entire train station ground to an immediate halt. Everything stopped, even more so than it had the night she'd realised Harry was the Jack. The entire world just caved in on itself until nothing was left but absolute silence. At the same time, life very much continued just as it always had, which meant that she clearly hadn't heard properly.

"He's what?" she replied.

"He's dead, sweetheart," Henry said again, clearer this time, but with so much agony choking the words that they couldn't be anything but true. "They found him yesterday. He's dead."

Then Charlie was there. Amy wanted to snatch her hands back from her father and throw them around the scruffy sleuth, but he wasn't there for her. He was holding the paper up, his face serious, working. Giant block letters beside his crooked frown spelling out MURDER SUSPECT HARRY POUND DEAD.

"This is true?" he checked.

Henry nodded, jowls and sideburns quivering. Charlie paused. A small breath of wind went out of his sails as he looked at them, torn, as always, between justice and compassion.

"I'm sorry…" he muttered. "Henry… Amy… I'm so, so sorry…"

Henry gave him a grateful nod. "Thank you, Mister Shilling."

It wasn't enough. It never was with Charlie. The crease of deduction narrowed his brow, and he looked sharply between them and the paper again.

"How much of this is true?" he pressed, subtly wiggling the rolled paper.

Henry's face fell. His lip quivered again, and Amy knew for certain she was going to cry again, she just didn't know if it would be this second or in the next few hours.

"To the best of my knowledge," Henry answered slowly, "all of it."

"Bollocks," Charlie cursed. "They've never gotten everything right."

"They know as much as I do," Henry insisted, raising his head stoically. "He was found hanging in his cell, from ropes knotted from his bedsheets. Monty had me verify the body."

"He was being kept in solitary. They really suspect no foul play?" Charlie pressed.

Amy wondered if this was how he coped. She was half numb, semi-detached from the world, absent of human concerns. Charlie wasn't. Not ever. He was always overwhelmed by human concerns. Maybe that was how he coped, by turning everything into work, by always focusing on the puzzle. Just like now.

"He did it to himself," Henry said quietly, with the deadly tone of grief only a parent could muster.

Charlie continued to frown. "I have questions," he announced.

"In that case, Mister Shilling, get in line," Henry advised. His tone was patient, but daring. Amy felt her heart break. Her father wasn't going to ask Charlie for help, but he was, like all of them, hoping for it all the same. There was a new mystery to solve.

Thus concludes *The Thief & the Marquis* Book Two of the *Shilling & Florin Mysteries*. The story continues in
BOOK THREE:
A DALLIANCE WITH GRIEF

Did you enjoy this book?

Please consider leaving a review for it on Amazon or Goodreads. Every positive review allows me to spend more time writing books for you to enjoy!

OTHER BOOKS BY KATE HALEY

Welcome to the Inbetween

The Light After Earth

Like the Heroes of Old

Shilling & Florin Mysteries

1. The Jack of Hearts Murders

2. The Thief & the Marquis

3. A Dalliance with Grief

4. The Case of Silver & Sovereign

5. A Cold & Bitter Revenge

6. The Pen & the Blade

7. Blood & Bells

8. Tarnished Silver

The War of the North Saga

Footsteps into the Unfamiliar (short story collection)

1. Steel & Stone

2. Magic in the Marshes

3. Forest of Ghosts

4. Women of the Woods

5. Spirit & Sand

6. The Prince and the Witch

7. Gods & Dragons

The Vincent Temple Trilogy (+ Prequel)

Path of Dreaming Souls (Prequel)

1. Gateway to Dark Stars

2. Tomb of Endless Night

3. Fortress of the Shadow Reich

ABOUT THE AUTHOR

Kate Haley is a speculative fiction author who works predominantly in fantasy and horror.

While currently content to fill their days with writing and table-top RPGs, their grander plans involve world domination. Something akin to the tyranny of the greatest city atop the Disc would be an acceptable standard. They believe a super-villainous overlord would be an upgrade, given that our current villains lack style and imagination.

After all, super-villainy requires Presentation.

If you like their references, consider visiting their website www.katehaleyauthor.com for short fictions and merchandise, and join the mailing list for early access and exclusive cool stuff.

You can also get in touch through the website regarding their work, your position in future slave armies, or a general interest in all things nerdy and wonderful.